A SECOND CHANCE

OTHER TITLES BY WALT MUSSELL

The Samurai's Honor
(The Heart of the Samurai Book 0)

The Samurai's Heart
(The Heart of the Samurai Book 1)

A

SECOND

CHANCE

Berta,
Hope you enjoy this!
Thank you!   W. Mussell

Walt Mussell

Copyright © 2021, Walter Edward Mussell

First EDITION

All rights reserved.

By payment of required fees, you have been granted the *non*-exclusive, *non*-transferable right to access and read the text of this Book. No part of this text may be reproduced, transmitted, downloaded, decompiled, reverse engineered, or stored in or introduced into any information storage and retrieval system, in any form or by any means, whether electronic or mechanical, now known or hereinafter invented without the express written permission of copyright owner.

Please Note

This is a work of fiction. Names, characters, places, and incidents either are the product of the author's imagination or are used fictitiously, and any resemblance to actual persons, living or dead, business establishments, events or locales is entirely coincidental.

The reverse engineering, uploading, and/or distributing of this Book via the internet or via any other means without the permission of the copyright owner is illegal and punishable by law. Please purchase only authorized electronic editions, and do not participate in or encourage electronic piracy of copyrighted materials. Your support of the author's rights is appreciated.

Cover Design by Killion Publishing

ISBN: 978-0-9992910-4-7

Published by Walter Mussell

For Andrew and Christopher, for whom I would do anything.

PLEASE NOTE

A Second Chance was initially released as *Second Chances* as part of the Love & Grace Boxed Set published by Gracepoint in 2016 to support a school in Atlanta for children with dyslexia. This story has been rewritten and expanded. The first version remains part of the original anthology.

AUTHOR'S NOTE

Though actual figures and events are mentioned in this book, the book remains a work of fiction.

If a full name is used in the story, contemporary characters are presented in Western convention of first name first. Historical characters are presented in the Japanese convention of last name first. For contemporary character Kira Sakamichi, this means Kira is her first name and Sakamichi is her last name. For historical figure Niwa Nagahide (a noted samurai from the period who appears in the book), his last name is Niwa and his first name Nagahide.

Single-term definitions are listed in the Glossary. However, I have mentioned three of them here below. In Japanese society, it is proper to use some polite form of address attached to one's name. The terms of address that arise in this book are as follows:

-sama – A term of address that shows respect to someone who is of elevated rank.
-san – The most common title. It can mean "Mr.," "Mrs.," "Ms.," and "Miss."
-chan - A term of address used for children. Also a term of affection within a family.

There are cultural references throughout the story. They are discussed in the Historical/Cultural Notes section after the story on a chapter-by-chapter basis. Consult this section if needed.

LIST OF CHARACTERS

Contemporary United States

Kira Sakamichi: Corporate Team Lead whose mother is always is "arranging" meetings with potential future suitors.
Mr. and Mrs. Sakamichi: Kira's parents. She refers to them as *Mama* and *Papa* with a Japanese pronunciation.
Kira's Grandmother: Kira's maternal grandmother. Always called "Grandmother."
Ted Tanner: Kira's co-worker.
Dr. Sanchez: Hospital doctor.
Stephen Igami: Son of a friend of Kira's mother and the latest attempt by Kira's mother to arrange a boyfriend.
Holly Sturges: Hospital nurse.

Medieval Japan

Ogawa: High-ranking samurai in the service of Lord Oda Nobunaga.
Lady Ogawa: Wife of Ogawa and mother of Mitsuyono.
Kira: Ogawa's concubine and mother of Shinnosuke.
Shinnosuke: Older son of Ogawa. Often called Shin.
Mitsuyono: Infant son of Ogawa.
Master Aoki: Head of a nearby monastery that Ogawa supports.
Igami: Monk/educator at a nearby monastery and private teacher of Shinnosuke.
Yutani: Teenage monk and trainer of novitiates at the monastery.
Nene: Older female servant in the Ogawa household.
Taka: Older male servant in the Ogawa household.
Niwa Nagahide: One of Oda Nobunaga's generals.
Haseda: Local magistrate.

List of Characters

The following list notes individuals from history mentioned in the book.

Oda Nobunaga: Feudal lord who unified half of Japan.
Hashiba Hideyoshi: One of Oda's generals. He is better known by the name Toyotomi Hideyoshi. He received the name Toyotomi in 1586 from the Imperial Court.

CHAPTER ONE

Kira Sakamichi tapped the speaker setting on her phone and then set it on the dashboard of her Escalade.

"Kira-*chan*, are you there?" her mother asked.

Kira checked herself in the visor mirror and brushed back her shoulder-length black hair. Still frizzy. She sighed and shook her head. "*Mama*, I'm here."

"Have you left work yet?" Like always, her mother's tone suggested she was hiding something. "Your grandmother wants to catch up on the latest two episodes of the Taiga drama. She wants you to watch it with her after dinner, like when you were a little girl."

A Taiga drama. Overblown samurai stories. Every year NHK, Japanese PBS, put out a new historical drama that ran once a week for the year. As a child, she'd watched them, first on video and then weekly when Kira's parents began subscribing to the Japanese-language cable channel. She sipped tea with her grandmother while her grandfather, a former history teacher, took joy in pointing out historical facts that the dramas portrayed wrong.

"It would mean a lot to your grandmother," her mother added. "She misses your grandfather so since his death. He loved these shows, too."

Kira could almost smell the chalk scent of her grandfather's fingertips as he would hand her treats, mingling with the sweet smell of the confections, her grandmother's perfume, and the aroma of the tea as they watched the shows. As a child, Kira had often dreamed of wearing beautiful kimonos like the women on television.

Not any longer.

Teen nightmares of her wearing a kimono out on the water had caused her to lose interest. Her grandfather thought it sounded like the Taiga drama *Yoshitsune* and the episode with the sea battle of Dan-no-ura. Watching the Imperial family, including the six-year-old emperor, drown itself to avoid capture. Kira was too young and fragile to see such a tragedy. A meshing of teenage fears that come with adolescence, the doctor had reasoned. She would grow out of them. She did, but occasional episodes would bring them back.

"I just got to the car, Mama, but I haven't left yet. I have to check a couple of things first."

A horn blast covered her mother's reply, the shrill blare not uncommon in her company's parking lot on a Friday. People hurried to get out early and beat Atlanta's Friday traffic walking in front of those already in their cars. "What did you say, Mama? I didn't hear you."

"I said it's important that you be here for dinner."

Her mother's tone raised her suspicion. "Mama, why is it so important?"

"Well"—her mother's pause let Kira knew she had her—"there's someone I want you to meet."

That explains it. Another one. Will she ever stop? "Mama, we've talked about this before. I don't need to find a boyfriend. My social life is fine."

"I've seen your Facebook page," her mother harrumphed. "Your social life sucks."

Kira imagined her mother in her usual pose, standing rigid with crossed arms and her patented disapproving glare. Relax. Start over. "Mama, customers and coworkers can see my social media. The posts have to be tame to protect my reputation."

"I know nuns who have more excitement. Please get here soon. He's the son of an old friend."

"I will."

Silence came from the other end. Was her mother giving in for now? Maybe. "I love you," her mother said.

"I love you, too. Bye-bye."

"*Ki o tsukete*, bye-bye."

Kira hung up and searched her console, then sighed in relief. It was there. Touch-up makeup for emergencies. She looked back at her visor mirror and spent a few minutes touching up her eyes and face, finishing with lipstick.

One last check.

Her hair remained frizzy. Nothing could fix this disaster.

A siren approached. Kira glanced toward the main road as an ambulance passed. Maybe her hair did not warrant that much concern. She checked her console again, finding a clip and putting her hair up. It would suffice.

She started the car and shifted into reverse. Her phone rang.

The number appeared on her screen.

Tanner. Damn.

She touched the green button. "Hi, Ted."

"Hi, Kira. Everything all right? You sound flustered."

Ted Tanner. The hardest worker on her team. She'd

thought him a total pain after management had assigned him to her, but Kira appreciated that he never missed a deadline. Married his high school sweetheart, put himself through college, and his wife already had a second child on the way. Loyal to his family first, but his 2:30 a.m. e-mails showed he got his job done, whatever it took.

"Yes, Ted. Everything's fine." She put the car into park. The sound of Ted's voice suggested the reason for his call wasn't good. "What's wrong?"

"Wood Designs called me. They're asking for a change on the project. We need to adjust the proposal we submitted an hour ago. Are you still near the office?"

"I—" Kira held her breath. She couldn't return now. With fresh makeup. People would notice. "There's a coffee shop at the next exit. I'll stop there and log back in. Talk to you in a few minutes."

She cut the call, backed out, and headed out of the parking lot. She was going to be late. Her mother would be disappointed.

###

Kira sped her Escalade down McEver Road, pushing the car as if the headlights would illuminate further. Revising the proposal had taken longer than expected. She had apologized to her mother when she left the coffee shop, the bitterness of the late-afternoon brews still on her lips, and said she would be there as soon as she could.

Her phone rang. She pressed the green answer button on the car display screen.

"Kira-chan, where are you?"

She sighed. "Mama, sorry. Traffic. I'm five minutes away. Ten tops. I'll be there soon."

"We are still eating. I have yours staying warm in the oven. I also made your favorite appetizer."

Dumplings. Her mouth watered at the impending

mix of pork and ginger.

Kira focused on the road. A pleasant drive on a sunny day. A mix of straight and windy sections with a bridge over Lake Lanier right before her parents' subdivision. Impressive homes to view. However, that was during the day.

At night, it was just treacherous. And near water.

Kira was thankful she had long since moved out when her parents bought their new place. Why did they have to buy a house on the lake? It had been years since Kira had experienced the nightmares, and she thought she was getting used to it, but sometimes flutters arrived that she couldn't quell.

Her phone beeped. She pressed her thumb to the side for security and glanced down at the message contents as she kept one eye on the road. Another question from Wood Designs. She could answer it as soon as she reached her parents' place.

She looked back at the road. A pair of yellowish eyes flashed in front of her.

Deer!

Kira veered right as she slammed on the brakes, the squeal cutting through the night. Her car plowed through the end of the guardrail.

White flashed. A slight whoosh followed by a paper bag pop.

Airbag.

The car rolled down the slope.

Toward the water. No! No! No!

The car hit the water, stopping upside down. Kira lurched side to side. Her head hit the window.

Spots filled her eyes, riding a wave of anguish. Water rushed through windshield cracks like a semi-blocked faucet, the spray chilling her face and clothes. She pushed the door.

Stuck.

She reached for the seat belt lock.
Her head swam with pain.
Then nothing.

CHAPTER TWO

Kira opened her eyes and flailed against the water. Her lungs burned for lack of air. She again reached for the seat belt lock.

It was gone. She was out of the car.

She pushed herself up toward the light, breaking the surface. Her mouth opened wide, her lungs gulping in a frenzy to fill her body with air again as she spit the mossy water taste from her mouth.

She was free. She was alive. *Thank God.*

Daylight? Impossible. It had been nighttime when she crashed into the water.

"*Okakasama. Okakasama,*" a child's voice called out.

Kira shivered, her teeth chattering, relieved that she had been thrown from the car. Pain throbbed in her temples. The chest-high water sloshed against her. What had happened? The car had gone in the lake. She had hit her head, then nothing else.

The water chilled her frame. She had to get out

now. A crashing of wood behind her drew her attention. She turned and saw a nearby dock. A raft tied to the end kept colliding with it. She searched for a ladder to climb out. Nothing. She turned left and her gaze followed the dock to shore. The only way out.

"*Okakasama. Okakasama,*" the youthful voice called again.

She rubbed the left side of head, feeling the bump, as she approached the shore. A light press increased the pain. She needed to get some ice and lie down. Her mother must be worried. She needed to call her now.

Her cell phone was in her hand when she saw the deer. She would never text and drive again. The phone must be in the car. How long would it take the phone to dry out in rice? Kira turned back toward the lake.

Where was the car?

This was not good.

Maybe she had the phone on her. She patted her pockets, both front and back. No phone.

No pockets.

Why was she in a kimono?

The bridge and trees that marked this spot were gone. So were the homes.

Kira's stomach fluttered. Where was she? This was not Lake Lanier.

Small hands pressed against her side. "*Okakasama. Okakasama.*"

Her chest tightened.

Okakasama?

Mother?

Why was a Japanese child calling her *Mother*? And why okakasama? Why not *okaasan, hahaue,* or even *mama*?

How did she know the word? She had never heard it before.

Tiny hands tugged on her arm. She looked down. A

little boy, around five or six, in a blue-and-white patchwork kimono, tears streaming from eyes that stared at her as if she were his only world. "Okakasama, are you hurt?" the little boy asked.

Shin. His name was Shin. Why did she know that?

"Yes, Shin—" She paused. Something was different. Either there or not there, she did not know which. "I am fine." She spoke in Japanese and heard the same. Her parents' tongue, though her mother had lived in the US since her own teen years. Kira had avoided studying Japanese as a child. Yet she now spoke it fluently.

And it sounded nothing like her mother.

The little boy threw his arms around her. "You fell in the water," he said, crying as he did. "I did not see you. I was scared."

Kira hugged the boy, then stood. The water level was above her knees and more than chest high on the boy. She glanced back at the dock. The boy thought she had fallen in. Had she lost her balance? What was she doing so close to a lake anyway? A stiff breeze sent chills through her clothes and whistles through the nearby woods. Her legs weakened and her breaths came in gasps. Her thoughts turned to Shin. "We should get out of the water. We both need to get warm."

They strode toward dry ground, Shin's hand in hers, her feet sinking in the mud. She moved her feet in the shallow water to rinse her toes as she reached the shore, stepped onto the grass to dry them, and turned back to the lake.

Her stomach fluttered again. She did not like being this close to water, but she had survived the fall. How close had this lake come to being her grave?

She glanced down at her feet and her gaze locked on the water.

Her reflection stared back at her, but it was not her.

A Japanese woman a few years younger than Kira, wearing a gaze of fear and relief. Kira reached back and pulled her hair forward. Instead of the shoulder-length style she knew, a long ponytail tied with a ribbon reached its tendrils toward her waist.

She tugged on the ponytail and grimaced. Yes, it was definitely her. Kira took a deep breath to quell the tremors along her skin. She then knelt and touched the water.

Ripples spread across the water and erased her reflection.

"Kira, are you injured?" a male voice called out.

Kira a man had said. It seemed her name was still the same.

She rose and turned toward the voice. A young, bald man in a gray robe and a brown bib, garments like that of a monk, raced toward her, blankets in hand. Likely in his late twenties, but he maintained an infectious baby grin. Monks did marry. Was this Shin's father?

No, her gut told her. A friendly acquaintance, but only that. No shared feelings of note, else she would know his name like she knew Shin's. The man threw blankets around them both.

"I am . . . just cold," she said through chattering teeth. "My head . . . hurts." Blood rushed through her body and she grew warmer. "My apologies. I do not remember what happened. I do not remember falling in the lake. I do not remember anything."

"Do you remember your name?"

She breathed out as if doing so released her ties to reality, but her name *had* remained the same. "Kira."

"Good. Do you remember my name?"

She studied him, searching for some recognition. "I am sorry, but no."

"Igami." He laughed, then beamed at her. "I saw

you fall off the dock. It looked like you struck your head when you fell. You disappeared underwater for a second and then reappeared. You and Shin should go back to the house. Have some miso soup and hot tea. You will feel better."

He picked up Shin and held him close. A thoughtful man, Igami, to look out for her son.

Her son.

Kira shook her head to shake away the sudden spots from her eyes. She had gone from understanding Shin was her son to feeling he was her son. Motherhood had never been one of her future goals. Yet there Shin was, Kira knew he was hers, and the connection tugged at her heart like a river current.

"Thank you for doing that," Kira said. She pulled her blanket tighter to hold the ends in her right hand and then rubbed her head with her left hand. The bump was still there. From the accident or from the fall? Were the events somehow the same?

Birds cawed from the nearby trees, then a rush of wings as several flew away. The fresh air different from what she knew. More changes from where she had been.

"Are you certain you are not injured?" Igami asked.

Chilled, moss-smelling lake water dripped down her face. "I did hit my head. My thoughts are a little foggy."

Igami tilted his head, his gaze focused on her. "Foggy? What do you mean 'foggy'?"

Kira stared. Igami understood the word, but the slang meaning confused him. She understood him fine. How could she? Her Japanese had never been that good. Yet, she was conversant here, wherever here was. "Like a fog," she responded, pulling the blanket tighter once again to protect against the breeze. "Like clouds inside my head. I cannot remember anything."

He nodded. "I understand. It must be a phrase from

your hometown. I have never heard it before." He gestured toward a large thatch house about thirty yards away. A smaller house, like a shed on stones, sat to the right, its front framed with a wooden fence that extended several yards toward the house. "You can explain more later," he added. "For now, get your sandals."

Sandals? "That would be good." She scanned the area. Adult and child-size footwear lay near the dock edge where it met the ground.

"Shin, come with me." They walked over and slid on the rice-straw sandals, the mixed smooth and rough textures strange.

"Good," Igami said. "We had better go inside."

She turned and looked at the water a last time, nodding at the reflection that mirrored her and then disappeared.

As if confirming her place was here.

A mist now danced on its surface, bubbling like the nausea that rumbled in her stomach, the feeling she often got near bodies of water. She stuck to showers when she could as baths made her nervous. Considering everything that had happened, Kira was as calm near water as she had ever been. When she had gone in, it was Lake Lanier. Where was she now?

That was easy. Japan. But not a Japan she had ever seen.

She turned toward the house Igami had indicated, staring at it and the others nearby. Old-style houses, but they appeared to be new. Like a film set or that tourist attraction in Kyoto that used to be a movie studio for samurai dramas. No power lines or any other wires. Nothing nearby either.

A simple dirt road was beyond the house. No cars. No bicycles. No horns or engines. Mountains in the distance. The Japanese countryside for sure, but even here she should see something. A few passersby walked along the road, carrying baskets on the shoulders. Most wore traditional dress. No jeans. No khakis. No boots. Nothing.

She gazed skyward. No planes. Nothing in the sky except for more birds.

Almost like she had gone back in time.

No. That was ridiculous.

The hair on the back of her neck rose as if tightening her throat so that she could not breathe. She was halfway around the world. Ridiculous was nothing compared to now.

Her wet hair and clothes clung to her frame. *Go into the house. Relax.* A change of clothes and some hot food would help her orient herself.

If only she had not lost her phone in the accident. She must be disoriented. She could call her mother. Mother must be worried to death. She would explain. Maybe there was a phone inside.

They soon reached the house. Igami slid open the door and showed them inside. A maid, an older woman with gray streaks peppering her hair, rushed up to them and bowed. She was clad in a dark beige kimono with a blue wraparound garment that appeared to be a cross between a skirt and an apron. The woman and Igami exchanged a few words, and then she took Shin with her, dragging Kira's heart along as the boy left. Was this the bond that mothers felt watching their kids? Any remaining doubts she might have had disappeared. She was Shin's mother.

Shinnosuke, she said to herself. That was Shin's full name.

But how was she here?

She rubbed her garments. Silk. Wet but no longer dripping. Likely ruined. Could any of it be salvaged? After she cleaned up, someone else could examine it. Later. After a call.

"Igami-*san*, do you have a phone? I apologize, but it is urgent."

Igami's face reddened while confusion filled his eyes. "You apologize to me? There is no need."

No need for politeness? "I understand. Do you have a phone?"

"Um," he said as he rubbed his chin, his eyes sweeping the room, "what is a phone?"

How could he not know about a phone?

Simple. She was back in time.

No, that was not possible. She understood his Japanese perfectly. She would understand the Japanese spoken back in time.

What was she saying? She could not speak fluent Japanese in any time.

"It is a machine. You use it to talk with people far away."

"Interesting." Igami's joyful smile returned. "I have never heard of such a thing, but I would love to see it. They have such a machine in your hometown?"

Never heard of it? The look on his face supported his belief. He did not know what a phone was. "Yes, Igami-san, it is common."

Confusion crossed his face again. "You keep ending my name with *san*. What is *san*?"

What is san? Is he serious? "It is a word of respect used with someone's name."

"I"—Igami shook his head—"have never heard the word. Only *sama* for respected people."

No san? It is always there in the movies. She rubbed her temple as her own confusion grew like an approaching storm. Had she really gone back in time? "Igami" —she stopped herself from adding *san*—"my head does hurt. I seem unable to remember some things. I have a childish question."

"Yes?"

"What day is it?"

"It is the tenth month of the fifth year of the Tenshō Era." He chuckled. "I do not recall the day."

Tenth month? It was cold for October.

No, not October. If back in time, then lunar calendar. More likely November. That explained the chill. "The Tenshō Era?"

Igami's face sported a somber tone. "Yes, the Tenshō Era, the name given by our lord, Oda Nobunaga."

Her knees shook. *Oda Nobunaga.*

The first of three men who united Japan.

Kira, welcome to the sixteenth century.

CHAPTER THREE

Igami left, saying he would alert someone to have food prepared for her and Shin and then return. The moments alone stretched like the dongs of a slow bell.

Kira rubbed her head again, but the pain remained. It could not be possible.

Oda Nobunaga.

How could she be here? When exactly was here? What did she remember from what her grandfather had taught her?

Nobunaga was assassinated in June of 1582. This was November, so it was not 1582 yet. Nobunaga conquered territory when? The 1560s and 1570s? She was uncertain. Many famous battles. The one with the guns. The Buddhist temple in Kyoto. She did not recall the dates. It would disappoint her grandfather.

Was he watching her now? How could he? He was not born yet.

A mixture of stumbles sounded from the back. Shin was a lively child. She needed to know him better.

But who was Kira? Her name was the same in both times. Was she from this time? Had she dreamed the future?

Not possible. The future had been too real. Foggy. Phone. She could not have dreamed those things. The future was her place.

Or would she forget the future? Would it soon seem like a dream? Was her life in the future dead? Had she died in Lake Lanier?

Was this reincarnation?

No, it was something else. Reincarnation went forward. She had gone back.

Was this a past life experience? Was she dying in the future and now seeing all her lives?

A trace of incense drew her toward a wooden box on a nearby pedestal. She peeked over the top, seeing incense burn in a squared pattern. An incense clock. An old way of telling time in Japan. Time moved forward, at least for now. But forward to what?

If only her grandmother were here right now.

Her grandmother had told Kira Bible stories as a child while her grandfather had taught her Japanese history.

What advice would her grandmother give her?

Pray to God, and the answers will come.

Kira glanced upward and let her gaze rest on the ceiling. What would she ask Him? Was Kira fully alive, dying, and already dead simultaneously? None of it made any sense.

Could Igami explain it? He was a Buddhist monk. He meditated on things like this.

Nothing was like this. How would she even explain to Igami where she had come from? The pain in her head increased. Would Igami believe her?

As if in answer, the monk returned to the room.

"Igami, I am fortunate you saw me fall."

Igami showed an embarrassed smile. "I try to watch you when you go to the lake as much as I can."

Watch her? "Why do you watch me?"

He stared at her. "Because you have always feared the water. But Shin enjoys it, so you approach it for him. I worry your fears may overcome you."

So this Kira feared the water as well, but she approached it for Shin, like any good mother would.

The patter of feet on the wooden floor hurried toward her. "Okakasama, hungry." Another servant, a middle-aged man, trailed him. The man wore a gray kimono with what looked to be a white one underneath and a simple obi around the waist. His bald pate rose out of cropped, graying hair. Sadness marked his face as he glanced at Kira and Shin.

Taka. That is the old man's name.

His lined face exhibited a mix of concern and regret. He bowed toward Kira and left.

"Okakasama, I am hungry," Shin said again.

She would think about what to tell Igami later. She had to focus on caring for Shin. Her son. That thought brought her joy, though her memories before today evaded her. *Sit tight and good things will come,* her mother always said, quoting the Japanese proverb. Kira would have to wait.

If only she had coffee. Was coffee available in this part of the world yet?

"Kira," Igami said, "you look ill. You should bathe and lie down."

She shook her head. "Not yet. Shin needs something to eat. You mentioned preparing food for him?"

"Yes, Master Aoki is visiting today. He is making something for Shin."

Aoki? The name sounded familiar, but she was still uncertain. "My a—" She stopped, reminding herself that

Igami had said there was no need to apologize. "Who is Master Aoki?"

"Master Aoki is the new head of my temple."

"I do not want to trouble him. He must have more important duties."

"It is no trouble. Before his elevation to head of our temple, Master Aoki worked in the kitchen. He has missed his time there." Igami brought his hand to his mouth, his gaze darting away as he flashed a light smile. "And his replacement is a much better cook," he said in hushed tones. "We have all gained weight since Aoki's promotion."

"I heard that," a voice called out.

Kira stifled a laugh. Before today, she could never recall meeting a monk, but she had always taken them to be as serene as the large stone Buddhas of Nara and Kamakura. The laughter now reminded her of one thing: Buddha often seemed to smile. Maybe she herself liked the kitchen in this place. Back home, she mostly ordered out or had it delivered. Her mother would approve of here more than home.

Another bald man in a gray robe and brown bib, a man about twice Igami's age and on the plump side with fat cheeks to match his bald head, stepped into the room. His robe carried splotches of food. A rice grain dotted his cheek, accenting his smile like a dimple. "Young monks like Igami have no appreciation for the subtleties of fine cuisine," he said as he strode forward. "Presentation is as important as taste. He will learn."

She allowed herself to laugh as Igami brushed the side of his mouth with his fingers. The older monk appeared puzzled before rubbing his own cheeks and finding the grain. He forced a sheepish grin, then downed the rice before resuming his feigned pompousness, which Kira now recognized as an act. The good cheer of these men offset the chill from the lake.

"It is wonderful to see you, Master Aoki."

"You must have hit your head hard, as Igami tells me," the older man said, studying her as he did. "That is the second time you have said that to me today. The first was when I arrived an hour ago. I agree with Igami. You should rest this afternoon, after you bathe and change into dry garments."

"I will get clean, but I need to look after him."

Igami shook his head. "After Shin eats, Master Aoki will take care of him. Then it is time for his lessons. I will see to his lessons after I get someone to take care of you." He turned to Shin and clapped his hands together. "Shin, go with Master Aoki."

Shin stood straight and bowed. "I will."

The young boy displayed an enormous smile as he rushed to the side of the old monk. Shin's expression suggested he enjoyed his time with both these men.

"Master Aoki, I am indebted to you for your kindness."

"It is nothing. It has been challenging for Shin with his father away serving Lord Oda. Now you go with Igami and I will care for him."

Shin's father. Not Kira's husband. Did that mean something?

Yes, Kira. It means you are paranoid and are reading too much into things.

A whiff of stale smoke filled Kira's nostrils. She leaned over to Igami. "Is something burning?" she asked.

He nodded. "Nothing to worry about. It is only the hearth. The nights are getting colder. You should get cleaned now. Come with me."

She nodded and fell in step behind the young monk, following him down the hall, its wood floor smooth under her feet. Floor hearths. She should have known. Was she expecting centralized heat? At least Igami did not mind educating her. Plus, he knew his way around the house. How often was this man here? Likely a lot.

"What lessons does Shin have today?" she asked.

He pivoted and stared. "Perhaps I *should* examine your head or send you to my temple to see our doctor. For you to forget this is concerning. For Shin, it is the same as always. His *kana*. He still reverses the characters of *sa* and *chi*, as if he is looking at them in a mirror. Other characters confuse him, too. I have never seen a boy as challenged as Shin. Frustrating, as he is a bright child. However, he is still young. I know he will learn."

"How do you know?"

His eyes twinkled like hazel highlights in deep brown. She could lose herself in them. "I come from a family of teachers. My parents worked wonders with children of other samurai. My father taught me everything I know." His continued gaze stirred her heart, as much as it had outside when he had rushed out with the blankets. "We will continue his education. It is only a matter of time until his skills match those of children his age."

So Shin had problems with reading and writing. Igami seemed confident. That was good. Too much to think about. She should rest. Then she would find Shin and see for herself.

Igami slid a door but motioned Kira to hold at the entrance. Likely a good idea. The floor of the new room had tatami mats. A hint of incense beckoned her inside, but her clothes were still damp. She needed to get clean first.

"I instructed Nene to bring a fresh kimono and undergarments for you," he said. "She left them in the bathing room."

Kira searched her memory. Nothing. "Nene?"

"The servant who took care of Shin when we came

in the house."

Of course. The gray-streaked maid she had seen earlier floated in her mind. Kira sighed. She could not avoid a bath any longer. If only this century had showers. "Where is the bathing room?" Her cheeks grew hot as she asked. Igami must think her foolish.

Igami's countenance betrayed no hint of criticism. "It is behind you. Nene said there is sufficient ash for washing. She also said she would return to help you dress."

Help Kira dress? "Will I need her help?"

Now his eyes opened wide. That question must have surprised him. "It is for the best, I believe."

Kira bowed, turned and took two steps, opened the door to the bathing room, and then closed it behind her. A modest heat greeted her face as she entered. The room was half the size of the one across the hall. There was one tatami mat on the left, where sat a clothing stand with what appeared to be fresh garments. She examined the garments. Dry white ones, likely for underneath, along with an orange-and-white patchwork kimono. She fingered the white garments and then held each one up, trying to imagine how they fit. Tattered, fraying, simplistic garments barged on her memory. Nothing like what she had here. She touched the kimono. Complex in appearance and cool to her touch. Igami was right. Kira would need Nene.

Another stand nearby held small white fabrics, likely for drying herself when done. An empty basket was on the mat to the right of the stand. A table was left of it. On it sat several vials.

The rest of the floor was wooden, though the far half of the room appeared different from the floor to her immediate right. In the far-right corner was a separate small room. What it held she would have to check.

To the left of the small room sat two large wooden

basins. Next to them were several buckets and what looked to be a small chair. Steam emanated from the basin, which was too small for a person.

She stared at the small, closed room. Was the bath in there?

She took a breath and opened the door.

No bath. Just a container on a pedestal, holding what looked to be hot rocks, likely from the hearth.

Steam emanated from the room. Just like a sauna.

Kira sighed in relaxation. In this house, to bathe must be to wash yourself. No bath to fear.

She disrobed, placing her wet garments in the empty basket in the front of the room, then entered the small room and sat for a few minutes to allow herself to perspire. She exited and sat on the chair next to the basins, feeling uneven as if she were leaning. She touched the water in each basin. One hot and one cold. She grabbed a wooden bucket and poured hot water over herself. The water moved to the far edge. That explained it. This half of the floor had a slight slope.

She glanced at the buckets. What did people in this period use for soap? Igami had mentioned ash. Another bucket sat nearby with a flat bamboo item on top. That must be it. She opened the bucket, scooped out the ash with the bamboo, and rubbed it on her arms and legs before putting it in her hair. The gritty texture felt like a sand bath, but it served its purpose as she scraped it off and doused herself again.

If only Mama could see me now.

She poured water over once more, then rubbed her skin and hair to check for ash. She touched the lump. Shards of pain coursed through her. She saw herself in her car, hitting the water and falling off the dock. Present and future merged.

The door slid open and Kira's breath hitched. She threw her arms across her body. *Igami?*

Nene entered and closed the door. "Are you ready?"

Kira nodded her head and rose as Nene grabbed one of the small cloths and brought it to Kira to dry herself. She marveled as she considered her ability to understand Nene's words. Different from Igami's and Aoki's polished styles. Folksy with a strong accent that Nene pushed to hide. Kira understood Nene's as well as she understood the monks, yet both sounded different from her parents and grandparents.

Nene helped her with the undergarments, which felt cool against her skin. "These are nice," Nene said. "It is good that you now have the lady's favor."

Now? Kira mulled over Nene's tone, a wave of joy in a lake of sadness. The mention of *the lady* meant *the lady of the house*, but whose house was this? Hopefully, she would know soon.

Nene extended one of the vials. Curious, Kira opened it and brought it to her nose. It smelled of walnuts. *Perfume?* She glanced at Nene, who looked puzzled then gestured as if Kira should douse her hair. Kira dabbed her wrists and ears.

Nene stared and shook her head, then held out the kimono, helping to slip it over Kira's shoulders. She fingered the garment. A fine cloth indeed. A slight tug on her head made Kira lean back as Nene squeezed out excess water and then ran a comb through her hair and tied it into a ponytail. Kira nodded to Nene to thank her.

Nene acknowledged her, but she looked troubled. The same sadness that marked Taka also affected Nene.

Kira thought it best not to ask.

She left the room and crossed back to where she was before, finally stepping on the tatami. Incense welcomed her entrance, and the *tokonoma*, the recessed alcove on the right wall, showed the smoldering remains of the scent that soothed the knots in her head and shoulders. She belonged here, even if she did not recognize it.

Igami stood there waiting on the other side of the room. He had arranged the bedding for her. He had taken care of everything. "Do you feel refreshed?"

"I do. Refreshed and relieved. The bathing room is nice."

"Yes, a luxury reserved for the wealthy or the inventive until one can visit a temple to properly soak in hot water."

Kira appreciated the explanation but mulled over what to say next. The other Kira must know what Igami just said. Did he suspect something? Was that why he mentioned it? "I"—she stopped herself from apologizing—"regret to have troubled you."

"It is no burden. The stress of Ogawa-*sama* being away for so long, fearing he may not return from battle, leaves an emptiness."

Ogawa? So that was the name of the head of this house. The smoky scent from the hearth in the main room reached her again, cutting through the incense. She was unaccustomed to it. Kira needed to be respectful in any discussion of Ogawa. She slanted her body to avoid looking directly at the young monk. "He is happiest when serving Lord Oda." She bit her lip, as if to bite the lie. She knew nothing about the man. However, a samurai would always be happiest serving his lord. Ogawa would be the same.

But who was he? Strands of a face with a hard jaw and striking eyes wafted through her thoughts. A handsome man, though older than Kira. Was she married to this samurai? Had it been an arranged marriage? Whatever had happened, Mama would be happy about it.

But some feeling was missing. Respect without love. Why?

Time to ask now. To know her official place in the

house. If she were Ogawa's wife, then that explained Igami's surprise at her deference to him.

"Igami, I need to ask you something and it may sound strange." She read his eyes and knew she could trust him. "You must promise never to reveal what I am about to say."

His eyes still glistened, but his posture turned serious. "You have my word."

"I did hit my head pretty hard. I must look a sight. Do you have a mirror? I would like to see myself."

Igami opened a closet and retrieved a box, withdrawing a mirror and handing it to her. Kira gazed at her reflection. Still the younger woman with the long hair, her face slender and ears small. She held the mirror above her head, glancing up as her left hand touched the bump. The red fabric tying her hair a nice complement. She brought the mirror back to her face for one last view, this sixteenth-century version of her more of a natural beauty than her modern self. She smiled and sighed.

"You look relieved," Igami said, sounding puzzled.

"Just trying to remember if I had blackened teeth," Kira responded.

He narrowed his gaze. "No reason you should."

Kira nodded, not knowing how thankful she should be. Did that mean she was high or low status? Time to find out. She handed the mirror to Igami. "How long have Ogawa and I been . . . ?"

The sparkle in his eyes vanished, replaced by a glare of a principal who had caught a misbehaving child. No wonder he made an excellent teacher. He returned the mirror to the box and then came back to her. "You really do not remember your place in this house, do you?"

She clutched her chest, then rubbed her head. "I should show you the bump. I do not remember."

He grunted. "You are his consort. You serve his wife and him."

"But my son?" She pressed the bump. More memories floated back. Of the birth and Shin's early days. Each flashback brought discomfort and elation.

Igami said nothing, instead bringing his hands up, showing his palms and outstretched fingers. He wanted to examine her and was requesting permission. She nodded as her breath grew shallow. Would he find anything? He stepped behind her and pressed his fingers on her scalp, the trace of incense on his robes calming her nerves. He pressed his fingers lightly on her scalp. More pain into her head and tingling through her body. "What is it? Do you see a problem?"

"Just examining you. These lapses of yours, they are strange."

He avoided the subject of Shin. *Ask again.* "About my son?"

"Shin is his son as well." He walked back around to stand in front of her. "Ogawa-sama purchased you from your parents, as Lady Ogawa was barren. Your first child did not survive his birth. Eighteen months after that, Shin was born."

"Any other children?" Guilt tightened her chest. She did not remember the first child, but it felt as if Shin was not alone.

"The gods sometimes favor us by putting misery from our mind. The bump may have done that for you. There was a girl two years after Shin, but she died at birth."

Kira fought back tears. She was not even this woman, but the thought of losing two children made her body weak. She wanted to sob herself to sleep and needed to lie down before she passed out. "It all seems like a blur now. Maybe I should be thankful for the bump."

His gaze conveyed deep concern. For her. He had comforted her before. Something, though, felt different.

"Those days are over, Kira," Igami said at last. "Ogawa-sama needed an heir. You gave him one. For now."

The finality of his tone weighed on her like a castle stone. "What do you mean 'for now'?"

He tilted his head. "You have forgotten that as well?"

"Whatever it is, yes."

"Lady Ogawa gave birth to a son two months ago."

Kira's heart clutched at her chest. The wife had a son now? Not good. No need for her. No need for Shin. In the Bible, Sarah sent Hagar and Ishmael away when Jacob was born.

When *Isaac* was born, Kira corrected herself. More forgotten lessons of her grandmother. More disappointments. When Kira got back to her own time, she vowed to go to church with her grandmother more.

If she got back. Japanese history differed from the Bible. Execution and suicide were more common than exile.

"Why have I been permitted to stay?"

"From what I have seen, Ogawa-sama cares for Shin. But when Lady Ogawa was in her fourth month, she instructed you to return to your parents with Shin if a son was born. When one was, I thought you would soon depart."

Bursts of images of a woman sitting up with a thick rope in her mouth. Long conversations with the same woman, trying to keep her seated upright and awake for several days, those talks punctuated by baby cries. Had Kira been there for the birth of Shin's little brother? "So did I."

"Is your memory coming back?"

"Wisps of it, like passing clouds obscuring a view."

"Lady Ogawa fell ill during the pregnancy," Igami added. "With Ogawa-sama off serving Lord Oda, you cared for Lady Ogawa. Your loyalty does you honor. She is seeing glimpses of her previous strength, which has allowed her to spend time with Mitsuyono. You should rest now. You will need it soon."

Mitsuyono. So that is the baby's name. Kira knelt by her bedding, finally close enough to examine it. In her head, she had expected a futon. This was a thin mattress-like material on top of the tatami, with a cover that looked like a cross between a kimono and a quilt. Her pillow appeared to be high and wooden and covered with a long, thin pad, likely for her neck. Her head swam with conflicting impressions. She craved to lie down, hoping she would awaken from this dream. The edge in Igami's words held her alert. "Why?"

"Because when Lady Ogawa is completely healthy, you will have to leave."

CHAPTER FOUR

"Ogawa-sama has returned." Igami's voice carried through the house as he stepped in from the entryway.

Kira's heart leapt into her throat and she paused from the sweeping she had been doing in the main room of the house. It had been one day since her arrival. She had hoped to be alert today, but last night had provided little sleep. Rotating nightmares of the accident in the future, speeding along the road and then hitting the water, along with flashes of her both running down a road and tumbling off the dock in this time. Like death in both worlds.

When she rose, chores seemed the answer. Kept her mind off her dreams.

By keeping herself busy, she had also hoped to avoid Lady Ogawa, but Nene had told her Lady Ogawa had left the house early in the morning with Mitsuyono. With Lady Ogawa gone, Kira had done her best to familiarize herself with the house as well as assist Nene. She had hoped to walk the grounds as well. Later.

Kira had expected Igami any minute for Shin's daily lessons. She had learned from Nene that the monk was always on time. "When did he return?"

"Last night. The forces returned from Tedorigawa." His face turned ashen and he smoothed his robe as if speaking wrenched his frame. "They have been counting their numbers after their battle with the Uesugi."

The sullen nature of Igami's voice conveyed the news that the battle had not gone well. Kira searched her mind. She had heard of that battle before. One of the shows she had watched with her grandparents. The details escaped her.

Igami's face conveyed he knew them.

"You sound as if the battle went poorly," she said.

He glanced at the floor. "Over one thousand of Lord Oda's men killed."

Yes, that was it. The battle of the Tedori River. Lord Oda had relied on guns. Lord Uesugi gambled on the river and waited for rain. When Oda's guns would not spark, his men retreated.

"Have you seen Ogawa-sama yet?"

"I have. He visited the temple this morning with Lady Ogawa and Mitsuyono. He gave long prayers for the men who died, donated money, and requested we honor them."

A noble request but concerning. He had gone with Mitsuyono and left Shin at home. "How is he?"

"He shows the scars of battle and the sorrow of losing comrades."

"Anything else?"

Igami glanced behind her and froze.

A looming shadow fell across her feet. The hair stood on the back of her neck.

Kira turned.

A hard-jawed older man with a shaved pate stood before her.

The man from her visions.

Ogawa.

"If you want to know how I am, you can ask me yourself."

She hid her gaze and fell to her knees, brushing her nose lightly against the tatami mat floor. The beaten straw smelled fresh, as if recently replaced. "Welcome home, Ogawa-sama. You have worked so hard. May I bring you something?"

"I wish to see Shinnosuke," he said. His somber voice carried the timbre of death, mixed with a tint of hope. "It has been too long. Where is he?"

Relief washed over Kira and she exhaled the breath with a *whoosh* that she hoped Ogawa had not heard. She had feared Ogawa might be ignoring Shin when she heard what Igami had said about the temple visit. Apparently not.

Igami stepped forward. "He is in the classroom. He works diligently every day."

"Does he still have . . . the trouble?" Ogawa asked.

Igami bowed his head. Red splotches streaked his face. "Yes. However, he is doing better. He has improved his ability to distinguish between the characters of *ah* and *oh*, but there is other work to do."

Ogawa fumed, and then his face softened. "I remember *ah* and *oh* confusing me when I was young. My father called me foolish. I learned. So will Shinnosuke. Will you promise me that, Igami? No matter the sacrifice, will you pledge to ensure that he learns?"

Sacrifice? The word carried the tension of finality. Or did Kira only imagine a weight in Ogawa's tone?

Igami's face stiffened and he bowed low. "Like my father before me, I serve any request of the house of Ogawa. My family's debt to yours. Your kindness to the temple. I am here for you."

Ogawa turned to Kira. "The same question to you. Will you promise to see that Shinnosuke learns, no matter the sacrifice?"

Sacrifice. Again that word. Again that tone. Again that request. Not her imagination but still unclear. Would she understand later? The commitment obviously meant much to Ogawa. She bowed again. "You have my word, Ogawa-sama."

"That is good to hear."

Ogawa motioned for her to stand. Kira rose and studied his face. Sweat beaded on his forehead as he struggled with a great responsibility. She saw the father in his eyes. Time with his child would lighten that burden. "Shall we go see"—she paused to make sure she said his full name—"Shinnosuke?"

"Yes." The man smiled.

Ogawa headed toward the classroom with Igami and Kira close behind. As they all reached the entrance, Ogawa rushed into the room, his steps as if on air. Kira and Igami followed.

"Father," Shin said, his face lighting up as he put his brush aside and rose from his desk. The boy ran to his father and bowed as he got close. "You are home."

Ogawa brushed his hand against his eye. Was that a tear? The warrior had a soft heart for his children. "Is there anything you would like to do?"

"Father"—Shin beamed at him—"can we walk the garden?"

Ogawa rubbed his chin. "Yes, I think we should walk it with your little brother as well. He does not know me well, since I left before he was born. I saw him for the first time only this morning. Will you help me get to know him? First, you finish your lessons. I will even stay and watch. We can walk in the garden then."

Shin's eyes danced like fireworks. "Yes, sir."

###

The lessons over, Ogawa took his son's hand, and they walked out of the room. The lessons had lasted a couple of hours, with Nene bringing tea and treats midway for a break.

Kira listened for the footsteps that soon faded away. "It is good to see them like that," she said to Igami.

"Ogawa is a more attentive father than most samurai I have met. Yet, after learning of Lady Ogawa's request to you, I worried for Shin when Mitsuyono was born, thinking he would ignore Shin in deference to her. For his first day back, he has not." Igami paused, as if considering his words. "The tear in his eye, though, surprised me."

"You noticed it, too?" She looked into his eyes. "I thought that to be joy at seeing his son."

"Yes, there is joy in his heart. However, I have watched Ogawa-sama for years. My father taught him when he was a boy. Long have I admired him. Revered him. He is an emotional man. This is different."

Different. Would that be the reason I came to this time? "How do you mean? How is it different?"

"Family has always mattered to Ogawa-sama, but duty is first. His manner now suggests family matters as much as duty."

"I understand." *I think.* "What garden is he talking about?"

Igami rolled his eyes but then shot her a glance that warmed her toes. Part of her wanted to leave the room and evade his gaze. Did he think her questions too foolish? Thankfully, not yet.

Shin's muffled shouts of joy sounded through the walls. Igami closed the entrance to the rest of the house where Ogawa and Shin had departed, then headed to the back of the room, sliding open the door. Chilly air gripped Kira, as the wind sped into the house. She pulled her kimono tighter and stepped onto the porch. A rock garden lay before her, divided with paths both through it and around it. The path led to the fenced building she remembered from yesterday, a smaller building set up with wide steps and a stone foundation to raise it off the ground. A path of flat circular stones led to the entrance, gentle footstones through a trail of tranquility.

"A tea house?" she said, staring at the structure.

"Yes. Ogawa-sama entertains there often. This tea house is the envy of many of Lord Oda's senior staff."

"Why is that?"

"Lord Oda decides who among his retainers has permission to perform the ceremony. Even Lord Hashiba is still forbidden."

Hashiba? The name sounded familiar, something her grandfather would be upset at Kira for forgetting. Hopefully, she would remember later. "So the tea house makes this a special place?"

Igami eyed her with amusement. "That and the bathing room. Though not unique, it is Ogawa's own design."

Kira nodded as she stepped onto the path for the rock garden. A wall to her left sheltered the tea house from the road and added to the place's solemnity, though a smattering of voices and the clop-clop of horses from the road disturbed the silence. She looked right, seeing the lake from which only yesterday she had emerged. Wind rustled through the trees while water lapped at the shore. Clouds cast darkness on the late afternoon, and torches leading to the lake had already been lit, likely for Ogawa and his sons to enjoy the evening. The light illuminated a structure, a boathouse of sorts, set next to the dock that jutted into the water. How had she not noticed it yesterday? The raft continued to float next to the dock, banging into it with a slow, constant drumbeat thud.

More flashes of memory. Shin and she at the

building on the lake. The scene was quiet, as if nothing had happened.

A chill reached her back.

Nothing *had* happened.

Yet.

Was something supposed to happen? Was that why she was here?

"Igami," she said, looking back, "what do you think Ogawa-sama meant earlier when he mentioned sacrifice?"

He looked down. "I do not know. He said the word twice. He asked each of us for a promise."

Kira's chest grew tight. She took a deep breath and held it. Igami knew more than he was saying. Was he afraid to tell Kira? What would that promise entail?

Why did it feel final?

CHAPTER FIVE

The next morning passed without incident. Ogawa spent most of his time with Shin and Mitsuyono. Kira had tried to keep quiet and listen for the voices in the house, but she had seen little of either.

However, she had finally met Lady Ogawa. The visit to the temple the previous day had tired her. She had grown weak and craved rest. With Nene occupied in other duties, Kira had brought Lady Ogawa her food. Her mistress had eaten little and then requested modest errands.

Kira had provided all.

What must it be like for a wife forced to depend on everything from a consort?

What a reminder to Kira of her position.

The time she had glimpsed Ogawa, he had remained the same. The mention of the promise not broached again. He neither looked her way nor addressed her, and his face remained solemn.

Lady Ogawa's face matched.

Kira understood not to ask why.

She focused on her other duties, as Shin was spending time with his father. She worked with other servants, ensuring that the house remained immaculate. There was scant else to do. With time available, she walked to the lake. Its draw on her pulsed like a heartbeat across generations, challenging her fear.

And stimulating her hope. Was there a way back?

At first, Kira had walked the grounds to get out of the house. Then she searched intently, seeking a doorway back to the present. None appeared. None but the lake.

The breeze swirled over it, lapping her with the scents of forest marsh and bamboo, dropping leaves and large twigs on otherwise still waters. Circles grew in all directions, bringing modest waves to the shore.

No other movement showed.

No images of a passage to the present.

Was the doorway at the bottom of the lake? Was that the only way home? If she found the right point, would the lake part to show her the way?

Or was she now here for good? Was her future to grow more like the woman into whom she had found herself? What had happened to the woman whose life she now occupied? Had she passed? Was her spirit now in the present?

Kira chuckled. How confused that woman must be.

Not confused, Kira realized. Frightened.

Easier to confront the past than to face the future. The past is familiar.

Sadness gripped Kira's heart. How would her mother handle whatever had happened?

But Kira was here now. Daydreaming would solve nothing. Work would not get her closer to the truth either, but it would keep her occupied until the reason for her being here presented itself. If only her grandmother were here, she would have some words of faith to allay Kira's fears.

She headed back to the house. Perhaps inspecting the front gate and the entrance would provide a new salve for her thoughts.

As she reached the front, the neigh of a horse announced a visitor. The gate opened. In walked an older man dressed in a fine gray *kataginu*, the kimono with wing-like shoulders, and pleated pants. Full samurai garb, down to the two swords. His thin black mustache and goatee framed his mouth. His pride and bearing in plain sight for all. A horse moved back and forth in the gate opening, its reins held by another samurai who remained outside and stoic.

The older man stared at her.

Panic gripped Kira, and she trembled as her chest flooded with pain.

What am I waiting for?

She hit the ground and bowed low. "Welcome. Welcome to the Ogawa household. How may I serve you?"

The man approached. His precise steps carried the weight of his authority. The horse nickers reached her ears, as the man's presence brought a mix of hay, sweat, and manure. "Tell your master that Niwa Nagahide is here."

"Yes, sir." She bowed again, then rose, avoiding his gaze as she did. She searched her memory for his name.

None.

It did not matter. His importance reigned over anyone who glimpsed him.

She entered the house and searched for Ogawa, finding him in the sitting room, telling the boys about the Ogawa family shrine. Ogawa held Mitsuyono on his lap and against his chest, while Shin made funny faces at his little brother.

Many samurai possessed the souls of a poet. Ogawa possessed the soul of a father.

He looked up at her, as if perturbed at the interruption. "Yes?"

She knelt and bowed. "Niwa-sama has arrived."

He nodded gently with a wistful gaze, as if he had expected the samurai's arrival. He rose and flicked dust flecks. "Nene," he yelled.

The older woman appeared, dressed in a brown kimono with hatched lines. Her tightly pulled hair lined with her now prominent gray strands. Nene had treated Kira well since her arrival, but she could not recall if they had ever been close. Like much around here that she could not recall.

Ogawa instructed Nene to take the children, his tone more of a request than a command. Nene cuddled Mitsuyono in one arm while clasping Shin's hand and took both boys out of the room. Watching them leave, Ogawa walked over to Kira. "Igami is in the classroom. I instructed him to be here all day. Bring hot water and my finest tea set to the tea house. Igami knows where my cups are. He will assist you. I will greet Niwa and escort him there." Ogawa's gaze softened further, and he placed his hand on her shoulder. A show of support. *For her.* "Be strong and remember your duty," he said.

Kira's mouth dropped open as she watched Ogawa leave. She might be Ogawa's consort, but his crossing of status boundaries made her head swim. This, and his request for sacrifice, what did it mean?

Kira found Igami, who was reading in the classroom. They put water to boil over the hearth fire and hurried to prepare trays with serving bowls and confections. It did not seem enough.

She brushed the smooth ash-colored ceramic bowls Igami had retrieved, admiring the intricate plant designs on each. There was also white-glazed pottery that resembled porcelain and had similar designs. "These items are beautiful."

"Yes, Lord Nobunaga convinced potters from nearby Seto to move closer and establish kilns here. Their work is inspiring. Ogawa-sama has other hues as well to match the different seasons."

Another notable facet of Ogawa's soul. "Who is Niwa-sama?" Kira asked.

Igami sucked in his breath. Kira had likely asked another silly question.

"One of Lord Oda's generals," Igami answered. "Like Ogawa-sama, he was at the battle at Tedori River."

"Does he come here often? I do not recall him at all."

"Still forgetful?"

"A little."

He inhaled through his teeth. "I have never seen him here, but that means nothing." He paused, as if considering his words. "I am usually only here in the afternoon. Samurai are early risers and, as I mentioned, Ogawa's tea house is famous among the elite samurai. Niwa-sama could have been here before, but I do not believe he has visited."

"Why do you say that?"

"I saw Niwa-sama once at the temple. He is an impressive figure. Even with your head injury, I could not imagine you would forget him."

Kira rubbed her arms, but a deep chill remained. "Why would he be here?"

He gazed at the ceiling, then back at her. Something was on his mind, but he hesitated to reveal it. "I do not know."

Concealing the truth. "You do know. It is written on your face."

"Written on my face?" He touched his fingers to his

forehead, chin, and cheeks, and then checked the tips. "There is ink on me?"

She laughed inside. Another colloquialism. She tried to hide it, but something in his manner relaxed her. "It is a saying where I am from. It means that I can see the truth from your facial expression. You know why he is here."

"You have strange sayings. I have never visited the district you came from, but I wonder how confused I would be if I visited there."

She stifled her laugh as best she could. How would Igami handle her time? Her home? Likely better than the woman whose life she had displaced. What would Igami think? No telling. "Many things are different where I am from."

"The water should be ready." He beamed, his gaze catching hers. That same glance that warmed her toes. "We can discuss later how things are different in your hometown."

Kira looked down as she grew light-headed. Did he mean to imply they might have time to talk? Later sounded like it would be too long to wait.

They carried everything out to the tea house, providing Kira a better chance to study the building. Igami was right. It was impressive. The stone base and steps, the single-piece timbers that served as the frame, and the intricate thatching of the roof were excellent construction. Her gaze then fell on the door, small and low. Its position required everyone to bow in order to enter. Both men's swords lay on a pedestal to the left. Another effect of the small door, and an indication that the inside was dedicated to peace.

Kira climbed the stone steps, taking the water and cups first and setting them down. She knelt at the entrance, slid the door open, and bowed low before she entered.

Niwa paid her no attention. Ogawa gestured toward a small hearth already lit with coals. She hung the water pot over it, set the tea and cups next to Ogawa, then bowed again and returned to the entrance.

Igami's face appeared. He placed the next tray in front of her, nodding but not daring to enter. She placed the treats next to the first tray, bowed again, and allowed herself to raise her gaze.

Intricate paintings of birds in flight decorated the walls. The tokonoma in the far-right corner displayed a calligraphy scroll. An elegant flower arrangement sat on the tokonoma's base.

Kira asked if anything else was needed.

Ogawa dismissed her without a glance.

She returned to the house with Igami while listening for sounds from the tea house.

Nothing but the chirps of birds.

They reentered the classroom. Shin waited at his desk, glee on his face.

Igami shifted his gaze between Shin and her, his care etched in his expression. The more time she spent here, the more she realized she cared for him. How much? He possessed a look that made her feel special. In another time, another place, would they know each other well?

Mother, could you not have brought home a guy like this? For this man, she would come to dinner early and stay late.

"You have no idea why Niwa is here?" Kira studied his face for a hint.

He paused, his eyes avoiding her. "None."

"You look like you do."

"It is written on my face, as you say." His smile broke the tension.

"I guess it is."

"Shin"—he turned away—"give us five minutes,

then we will begin." He pointed Kira back out the door.

"What is it?" Kira's heart skipped, sending twitches through her chest.

"Say nothing for now. After Niwa-sama leaves, I will request permission from Ogawa-sama to continue the afternoon's lesson at the temple, as it is only a short walk from here. It has been a while since Shin has visited. I will say it is an educational tour. I will also request your presence and promise to see the both of you home, as I am certain it will be dark when we return. Will you come?"

"I will."

"Good. I will find you later. For now, I must see to Shin. Prepare an extra kimono for each of you, as it will probably be cold this evening when we return. Ask Nene for help."

She watched him walk toward Shin, his strong gait etched with purpose.

Her thoughts and wishes flowing with him.

###

"Shin seems to have enjoyed the tour," Kira said, as she watched her son head away with Yutani, a tall, thin teenage monk who needed to shave his head again and pop a couple of pimples. He requested Shin help the other boys clean the room where visitors gave donations. Shin's excited response showed he enjoyed chatting with the teenage monk as well.

"Nice young man, that Yutani," she added, "and Shin seems to like him."

"Yes, he is good with children. He trains boys Shin's age in the basics of our order and is an older brother to them. We have many novitiates here. They are the future of the order."

"You do not look that old." She looked around, noting several children about, their haste increasing the floor squeaks. Children started young here. Had Igami started the same way? Likely. "I thought *you* were the future."

"No, I may be future leadership, but children are the future lifeblood."

She bit her lip, glancing around to see if anyone was nearby. No one. The incense that permeated the walls, both fresh and stale, calmed her nerves. It was time. "I have something I need to ask you."

"Yes?" Igami's serene look gave her no hint he would answer now.

"What are you hiding?"

"Hiding?" He stared at her, his eyes wide with puzzlement.

"Not telling me."

Comprehension lit his face. "Ah. You and your strange phrases again. They are confusing. It is like you have become a different person since you fell in the water. I cannot explain it, other than the words you use, but you are as new as undyed silk."

"What do you mean 'new'?"

Two children ran through the area, their feet slapping the floor. Yutani entered the hall and chided them to slow and show respect. The children walked toward Yutani and made an apologetic bow.

Igami gestured toward the children and Yutani. "Like a child, though you are an adult. Like someone from another land who has stepped into a realm she understands not. You resemble those foul-smelling traders from afar who travel with the dark-clad religious men who call themselves *Kirishitans*. They are learned in their own land but like children here."

An excellent description. Could she tell him? Should she tell him? Would he think her mad?

Do I have a choice?

She moistened her lips and stiffened her frame. "I am . . . different."

"How?" His brown eyes fixed on her, sending heat to her face. "You are almost a different person. You have some of your memories, yet you behave as if your memories belong to another. It is as if a spirit has taken you."

Her heart beat faster. She lowered her gaze to hide the truth in her face. "A spirit? That may be true. Do you think it is an evil spirit?"

"Walk with me and I will answer your questions."

Kira dropped a step behind and followed him to the large wooden gate at the front of the temple complex. He pointed to the entrance. "Do you see the statues?"

Kira moved closer and studied the two wooden figures. Each was roughly ten feet tall. Warlike fierce yet somehow friendly, at least to her. Ominous to all who entered with ill. Both the same but with one exception. Left side male with mouth closed. Right side female with mouth open. *Kind of like my parents.* Igami sidled next to her. She glanced at him. "They look familiar."

Igami laughed. "That is true. The artist modeled them after the ones at Tōdai-ji in Nara. Once you see the ones at Tōdai-ji, you never forget. Have you ever visited Tōdai-ji?"

She remembered only one building from when her relatives took her to Nara. "The place with the big indoor Buddha?"

Igami laughed. His smile broke her tension. "Yes, that is it."

"Why are the statues here?"

He steepled his fingers, almost as if taking the role of a teacher. "They are here for the same reason as any other temple. They are protectors. The beginning and end of life. They scare away evil spirits and allow the good ones to remain. They allowed you on the grounds." He crossed his arms and again flashed the grin that weakened her knees since the day she had risen from the lake. "The spirit within you is not evil."

"What remains?"

"Rebirth. We believe in it, but the gods blessed you with it. I have yet to meet anyone who recalls a past life, but I believe you do."

Kira considered her next words. Her grandmother would tell her to trust in God. Igami's earlier mention of Christians must be a sign.

"I remember another life, but not from the past."

Igami's mouth opened and he stared at her.

"Are you all right?" Kira asked.

He exhaled and stared blankly into space, shaking his head. "For this, I need tea . . . and Master Aoki. Come."

"Wait"—she glanced about the grounds but saw little movement—"what about Shin?"

"Shin is under capable supervision. We will find him after we talk with Master Aoki. Come now."

###

Kira sipped her tea, her thoughts wandering to Shin. Igami was right. Shin seemed to take to Yutani. For now, her son was fine.

Master Aoki chatted with monks who kept seeking his attention, delaying the discussion Igami suggested they have. Aoki and the monks kept their voices low. Temple business. Not for outsiders. Yet the monks glanced in her direction as if in support with eyes wide. Everyone knew something she did not.

Aoki's office was functional. A table placed in the center for meetings. A desk on one wall for Master Aoki to work. A few shelves filled with volumes, either writings or records, on another wall. A small lacquer chest with drawers, likely for incense, sat on a table next to the shelves. The office's only window separated the two. Incense burned on a nearby stand. Two scrolls decorated the wall opposite the desk, while the remaining walls were blank.

Aoki said goodbye to the other monks and then closed the door and invited Igami and her to sit on the floor at the table. "My apologies for the wait. Igami said you remember a previous life since you fell in the water, but a life not from the past?"

"Yes, but I only remember glimpses of my life here. The life I recall is the one from the future."

Aoki crossed his arms and looked down his nose at her. "From where?"

That is a good question. How do you explain a country that does not yet exist?

Directionally.

"I am from a land across the great water to the east. That is where I live in my time."

"The east?" Aoki closed his eyes. Was he praying? He opened his eyes, his brows rising high. "I see. You live with the southern barbarians on the other side of the world? I have heard a rumor that if you travel far enough east, you can reach their land. It sounded like fantasy. Are you not Japanese in your other life?"

Foul-smelling traders? Southern barbarians? The Portuguese in the sixteenth century created a reputation. How to explain? "My family is from this country, but I do not live where the traders do. Between here and there is another land mass. East of that land is another great water. Cross that second great water and you will find the . . . barbarians. The land between the two great waters is where I was born."

Aoki leaned forward, scratching his jaw as he did. Did he believe her?

Would she believe her in his place?

"What is this place called?" he asked.

Best to keep it simple. "It has more than one name. Its kanji name is *Beikoku*."

"Rice country? It sounds like a place I would like to

visit."

"It does not exist yet. My grandfather always told me the name was an accident, but I do not remember why."

"Why did your family leave here?"

A long subject. "My family moved there for work and marriage. Sometimes you must do what you can for your family."

Aoki sighed. "If we had time, you could draw me a map. I have many questions, and I wonder if I should know the answers." He inhaled like an eye-cutting wind. "However, time is short."

Short? Again, the finality.

"How did you find yourself here?" Aoki continued, "In *this* time."

Driving a car and running off a highway? How to explain? She glanced at Igami, his kind, soft eyes urging her forward. *Continue to trust. Lord, please guide me.*

"I was riding in a . . . cart. I was heading to my parents' home. It was dark. Cold. A deer appeared in the darkness and the cart went sideways to avoid a collision. The cart slid down a slope into a nearby lake and I fell unconscious. When I woke up, I was here."

"What is your name in the other time?" he asked.

"Kira, the same as here."

"Do you have a family name?" Aoki asked.

"Sakamichi."

Aoki chuckled. "Appropriate. I believe you. Your name means slope and includes the kanji for a road. Your name portends your future and your past."

Kira went numb. Was being here always her destiny?

Aoki braced himself, putting his hand to the floor as he stood. His frame seemed to shake from an unseen force. He grabbed a sip of tea, opened the window, and stared outside, his body stiff as the chilly breeze that flowed through the room.

"Woman of the future," Aoki said without turning, "have you enjoyed your time here?"

His tone was weighty. Ominous. What did he and Igami know that she did not? "Yes, do you think I will return to my time soon?"

"That is uncertain, but Niwa's visit to Ogawa today was no coincidence. There have been rumors about the battle at the Tedori River, questions on Ogawa's performance there."

"He was a coward?" Kira pressed into her chest as her heart pounded against the surface. It could not be true. Nothing about the man suggested any hint of fear, any hint of cowardice.

"I cannot imagine such. I would not believe it if I heard it. But rumors have been flowing back to us for several days now, rumors that suggest he should have died there or his decision led to the death of many men. Yet he survived."

"And came home." Kira thought about the house. Nene and Taka were always polite but never seemed to smile. "Do the other servants know?"

"Likely," Igami said.

"So he is in trouble because he is alive."

"Yes," Aoki added, as he turned toward her, "and because he is, Ogawa-sama has been judged by Lord Oda. Niwa delivered the decision. Ogawa's line is to die."

Kira swallowed hard. "His line? But that would mean . . . "

Aoki's lips thinned as pain crossed his face. "Yes. Him. His children, and any potential future children."

Kira's throat constricted, and she struggled to breathe. She was not pregnant and had not been with Ogawa since his return, but that would not matter.

She had come to this time to die.

CHAPTER SIX

The walk back to the house had taken only a few minutes but had felt like an hour. Darkness had long fallen before they had started. Only the city torches provided any light on the cloudy evening.

Kira craved to hold Shin. To run away with him, hide him, and keep him safe.

She stayed on her predetermined path.

Several times she glanced about. Samurai dotted the streets. Were they watching her? Why would they? She was of low importance. Yet all their eyes seemed on her.

At least Igami was here. His presence calmed her fears.

They soon reached Ogawa's house. Kira sent Shin inside, leaving Igami and her alone. She scrutinized him, yearning to have his arms wrapped around her, hold her, tell her this was all a dream.

If she woke, he would not be there. If she stayed in the dream, she would die.

Voices sounded from the street, growing louder as they passed. Kira remained silent until they faded. "What do I do?"

Igami exhaled a low breath. "One can delay one's fate in life, but escape is impossible."

She bit her lip. "What does delay do for me?"

"Time." His gaze grew soft and supportive. "Delay provides you time."

"What does time give me?"

He leaned forward, his lips almost brushing her ear. "Acceptance. Acceptance and hope."

"Is there truly hope?" she asked.

"There is always hope when there is meaning in death. You will know when it is time."

Another murmur of voices pierced the air. They were being guarded.

Her blood rushed to her heart. She wanted to hold him once again.

As she might have held him before.

Before.

She could not hold him now.

She had held him before? In this reality or in another time?

Whatever they shared, Ogawa was not aware of it. She and Igami would both be dead otherwise.

"I have a question, Kira of the future."

"What is it?"

"In your time, is everyone here called *san*?"

"Yes, though there is still a place for *sama*."

"Even children like Shin?"

"Shin would have a different name. He would be called"—she felt herself smile—"Shin-*chan*."

"Why does that make you laugh?"

How would she explain the well-known manga character? "In my time, there is a story of a mischievous Japanese boy. His name is Shin. The story is popular throughout the world."

"Even with the barbarians?" His eyes opened wide.

"Yes, even there."

"Thank you. Rest well, Kira-*san*. I will see you tomorrow," he said.

She gave a bow and watched him leave, knowing every second was precious.

Kira entered the house and looked for Shin. She found him at Ogawa's feet, listening as Ogawa related some historic tale. A tale of honor. Shin, normally blessed with a smile, maintained a stoic face.

Like his father.

Ogawa glanced at Kira, rubbed Shin's head, and sent him along.

She yearned to run to Shin and spirit him away. Yet her feet remained locked to the floor as if shackled. *Do your duty.*

Not that fleeing would get her anywhere.

"Kira," Ogawa began, "you do an excellent job raising our son."

She bowed. Praise from her master. There was no higher compliment. "You honor me with your praise." *Are his words preparing me for something? How to respond?* "Your leadership of this house is the reason he does well."

He laughed. "Were it another day, I would agree with you. Today is not that day. Sit."

Kira's shoulders stiffened. Sit? He asked her to sit, as if she were his equal? Even as Shin's mother, she remained unworthy.

To have these thoughts, I really have gone back in time. In body and in spirit. Mama would laugh.

She sat on the tatami, feeling the smooth straw on her fingertips. "How may I serve you, sir?" she asked.

He knelt and sat back on his feet. "Have you heard the rumors?"

She wanted to say no and hope Igami was wrong, but she could not lie to the man in front of her. Never had.

Nene entered, bringing tea to Ogawa. She then offered a cup to Kira.

Her breath came in quick gasps. Kira tried to calm her shaking hands.

She looked in Nene's eyes, eyes stained with the remnants of tears. She had long served this family.

The heat of the cup warmed Kira's chilled fingers. Nene left the room and Ogawa repeated the question.

"I heard," Kira said. "Has Lord Oda given the order?"

His shoulders slumped, as if the news weighed on him like a mountain. "Not formally."

"But it will be." A question not rhetorical, but one that needed no answer.

"There is a meeting midmorning tomorrow where we must present ourselves. No one expects us to be there. Until then, we have time to invoke our own deities and demons."

The pit in Kira's stomach pounded like a temple bell. "Shinnosuke and Mitsuyono? Is there no chance they will be spared?"

He smiled, as if to offer whatever his heart could open. "They will be reborn. May they be reborn samurai. I only pray that I may watch them grow in the next life. You remember your promise, do you not?"

The word *sacrifice* resonated in her head, like it had before. She would honor her commitment. "Yes, I will remain faithful to you and to my word."

He rose and knelt beside her, placing a hand on her shoulder, again patting her in support. How could a warrior's touch be so gentle? He leaned in and kissed her on the cheek. "Keep your face and expression still. There is always hope when there is meaning in death. You will know when it is time."

The same words as Igami.

Ogawa rose and left, his gait slow and dignified.

A gallant man indeed.

Silence pervaded the house. A quick glance out the window in her room confirmed her suspicions. Two samurai remained on guard at the street entrance, ready to escort everyone for their sentencing tomorrow. Kira's stomach quivered. Was this feeling what prisoners on death row experienced? Or were people who committed a crime less nervous when it came time to pay for their deeds?

How about soldiers on the eve of a hopeless battle? In some ancient battles in Japan, when the ultimate day approached, the winning side sent entertainment for the losing side to enjoy on their last night alive.

Another servant, one who she had seen in passing but had avoided since she could not recall her name, had brought Kira dinner earlier. It had mattered not. Food offered strength only with the desire to eat. She possessed no desire at all. This would be her last night here. Her last night on earth. Her last night alive. No chance to see her parents and grandparents again.

Her grandmother's words came to her. *In prayer, there is strength.*

Kira closed her eyes. *Lord, please see me through this. Please give me strength.*

"Do you regret your decision?" Lady Ogawa's voice startled her.

Kira scrambled to her knees and bowed. Lady Ogawa acknowledged her with a nod and intimated she should rise. Mitsuyono, nestled in Lady Ogawa's arms, suckled at her breast. Motherhood. She had no children in the future and had experienced only a few days of it here. Yet she had bonded with Shin. If only she could recall how the real Kira had felt over the years with Shin. No wonder her own mother worried so. The bond was eternal.

"My decision?" Kira said. "My lady, I have no regrets."

Lady Ogawa smiled. "You maintain your thoughts well. We brought you here to provide my husband with a child when I could not."

What Lady Ogawa must have endured. To watch another woman produce a son for her husband. To see that son every day, the resemblance to her husband and his consort. Lady Ogawa possessed remarkable fortitude. "I serve the Ogawa family, including you. I take your orders and his."

"Yes, you do." Lady Ogawa stared down at her son. "Before Mitsuyono was born, I told you that you would need to take your son and leave if I gave birth to a boy."

Images of the conversation flooded back like a lake tide. She was embracing the Kira of this time more and more. "I remember, and then you fell ill before your son's birth. I could not desert you."

"It may have been better if you had left." The woman's gaze bored into her. "You might not face our fate."

Heaviness like a mountain descended on her heart. Her place was here. "I made the right decision." What reason could she tell that Lady Ogawa could believe? What reason would convince her?

Duty. Ending shame.

"Once my parents sold me, I could not return to them. They would disown me for abandoning my master. I serve this family. This family's fate is my fate." She steeled her nerves. "I will meet it well."

Lady Ogawa eyed her up and down. Did she believe Kira? Did it matter? They would all be dead tomorrow.

"You do not deserve the name I gave you."

Kira froze and stared at Lady Ogawa. "You gave me?"

"You have forgotten that as well?" She grinned and held Mitsuyono tighter. "That fall in the lake did affect your memory. For that I am thankful and embarrassed. I gave you the name Kira. You were like a new toy to my husband when you first arrived. Like the sparkle of the sun on water. *Kirakira.* It is why I ordered that you wear dingy, faded garments when you first arrived, only relenting on days when my husband spent the night with you."

That explained the images from her first bath here, the unfamiliar fine clothes. "I have scant memory of that."

"For so long, I believed you to have no substance."

The shuffle of feet sounded in the distance. The house was busy tonight. Putting things in order. "What do you believe now?"

"You proved me wrong." Lady Ogawa licked her lips, as if considering her next words. "I felt remorse when you lost your first child and allowed you better garments. Then came your treatment of me when I fell ill. From there, I demanded the best for you. For your actions, the next world will surely reward you with favor."

Kira bowed once again. Lady Ogawa nodded and left, cradling her son.

Compared to this time's Kira, Kira herself was shallow and flashy. She thought of her parents, who had always been there for her. Of her promising career. Of her education.

Of her blessed life.

Maybe the next world rewarded me, only I did not realize it until now.

CHAPTER SEVEN

"Okakasama," Shin's voice cried when he saw her. "Everybody sad. Why?"

The last two hours had passed slowly. It was well beyond Shin's bedtime, but that simple convention did not seem to matter. After Lady Ogawa had left, Kira had prayed, seen Shin, then sent him back to his father and prayed again. Now Shin was back.

What should I tell him?

"Shin, you must be brave, and you must do what I tell you. Things will be better. Trust me. Things will be better."

"Do you promise?"

Kira's lips tightened. "I promise."

She put Shin to bed, telling him she would join him soon, and brushed his hair until he fell asleep. From there, she repaired to the classroom. Would she sense Igami there? He spent so many hours there his spirit likely lingered when he returned to the temple. Would it remain here with no students to teach? She surveyed the room, knowing it might be the last time, then opened the door that led outside.

Her last night alive.

A chilling wind cut through her clothes, but it invigorated her as she gazed across the rock garden at the tea house. She grabbed a pair of shoes and eased down the steps, turning right toward the lake. Owls hooted from the nearby woods, as if beckoning her to approach. Small streams of moonlight pierced through the clouds and reflected off the water.

Her heart skipped a beat and she halted.

Even with death imminent to her, the water brought fear.

Kira shivered, as if icy fingers traced her spine. Death approached on her own terms. If only Igami were here to put his arms around her and keep her warm.

If only she had more than one night remaining.

She gazed again at the water. Still no sign of a passage back home. If one opened, would she be able to take Shin? Likely not. If not, she would not leave him alone here. To face death.

Guttural voices sounded from the street. Late-night revelers likely headed home.

A place she would never see again.

Mother, I hope to see you again someday and prove that you raised me right.

Her eyes grew heavy with tears, despite the breeze that cut across her face. Time to retire to bed. Time to see Shin.

A rustle in the bushes drew her attention. A slender figure.

Yutani? Why would the young monk be here?

It could not be.

Whispers. Voices. Was she hearing things?

She circled back to the house, pressing her body against the side and in the shadows. More whispers.

More rustling.

Then nothing.

The boathouse near the lake appeared dead in the distance, except for the raft that still floated in front, slapping against both water and the structure.

Along with the faint cries of yesterday.

Was she hearing things?

Kira exhaled and rubbed her chest. Unfortunately, the tension remained.

Of course it did. One must face one's destiny.

More voices sounded around her, some from the street and some just on the air. Did one's senses become more acute at the approach of death?

She reentered the house and headed to her room. Shin slept silently on the floor, a smile on his face that seemed to grow wider as she approached. She rubbed his hair again, lay down, and closed her eyes.

Loud noises roused Kira from her sleep. She rushed to the window and slid it open.

Smoke billowed in, the stench filling her nose and stinging her eyes. She fought to see the smoke's direction.

The tea house!

A fire caller yelled orders, directing others around the ends of the wall that separated the rock garden from the road. Bells and knocks sounded from the front of the house. *The door.*

She roused Shin and took him in her arms, leading him to the front. Other servants ran about, calling out for Ogawa.

Ogawa-sama, where are you?

Kira slid open the door. A dour-looking man in a dark kimono and red face to match pressed into the house without introduction. "Where's Ogawa? His tea house is on fire."

How to answer? "We are searching for him now."

"Help the servants. Help put out the fire."

She set Shin on the front porch, finding a blanket and wrapping it around him, then ran to the tea house. There she found men digging a trench, while others brought buckets.

"Is anyone inside?" Kira asked.

"We do not know," one man responded. "The fire was too high. We could not go in. We must contain it here. If it spreads, we could lose both this house and nearby ones."

People arrived with buckets. Men formed a line between the lake and the tea house, bringing water to douse the flames. She scanned the line. Igami, Aoki, and Yutani along with other faces she recognized from the monastery. The monastery was close, but how did they hear of the fire so quickly? Could news travel this fast? Did the chanters that stand on street corners to raise temple funds somehow pass the news to them?

Or did the family's fate have the monks already watching them, ready to serve when death came?

A light drizzle started falling and chilled her skin but muffled the stench of smoke. Smiles broke out on many of the faces of the men on the bucket line. The rain would make the fire harder to spread and would spare the rest of the neighborhood. She wished she could bring hot drinks to the people. What could she do to help?

She ran to join the line. If this was to be her last night on Earth, let her spend it helping others. If only she could find Ogawa and his wife.

She looked at the burning tea house. Her throat tightened like a drying leather belt and she held her breath to stifle the cry that threatened to erupt.

No, not there.

CHAPTER EIGHT

Dawn peaked over the lake, bringing rays of warmth, yet too little to warm her frame.

A stale stench of smoke remained. The combination of men and rain had contained the fire. The smoldering coals provided heat and kept the officials away from her and other members of the house.

Not long enough.

An official in brown walked over to Kira, his face stern and eyes piercing hate. He wore a club in his belt. The bruises and scars on his face and arm suggested he would not hesitate to use it.

"My name is Haseda. I am the magistrate."

She bowed. "How may I help you, Haseda-sama?"

"You did not join your master and his wife?"

Did not join? Her fears from last night were true. Despite having hours to think about it, the news still struck her heart with the weight of ten rice bushels. "You found them?"

He smiled, his dark smile a mixture of grit and

grift. "We did. They took the honorable way out. They should be reborn to their same station."

"Ogawa-sama was an honorable man."

"Yes, he was." Haseda spat on the ground. "You should follow his example. Ogawa was samurai and deserved ceremony, but everyone is too busy for the likes of you. If not for Ogawa's position, I would strike you down now." He spat again. "Save us the trouble. You have already taken more time than you deserve. I have other business to address and will return in two hours."

The man walked away. His disdain for her trailed in his wake. He was right. She should be dead already. Perhaps back in Lake Lanier she already was.

So why had she traveled here?

"How are you this morning?" a familiar voice asked.

Kira turned, the surprise ebbing as an irritated smile forced its way to her lips. "What kind of question is that, Igami? How do you *think* I am doing? How would you feel in my shoes?"

He gazed at her with a puzzled look. "Your shoes?"

"Another expression used where I am from. It asks you to consider how you would feel if you faced my fate."

"I see. I will miss your expressions. If I faced the same fate as you, I would focus on my duty."

"Like Ogawa?" Her eyes teared. "They found him and his wife."

He nodded. "Yes, I heard. They committed *seppuku* and torched the tea house."

"Why?"

"To protect themselves in death."

"What about Mitsuyono?" she asked.

"Once the ash cools further, they will sift through the debris." Igami turned and looked toward the ruins.

"Mitsuyono was small. They may find nothing, but my temple will treat the ashes with reverence and make the proper arrangements."

Tears flowed from her eyes. "I cannot imagine the pain they endured. To die in those flames."

"Only Ogawa-sama would have experienced it, I think. Lady Ogawa would have done her duty. He would have spared her further pain, his family further pain, before setting the place on fire and then taking his own life."

Taking his own life. By slitting his stomach. "Why burn the tea house?"

"Revenge. To prevent those who called his honor into question from using it."

Kira cried more tears. The entire family. Poor Mitsuyono. His only crime was the name of his father. What kind of society required such a sacrifice? "And the same fate awaits Shin."

"Do not despair," Igami said. "There is still hope. For now, rest and enjoy your last meal."

"I have two hours before the magistrate returns. How can I rest?"

"You must rest. You need your strength. It is not yet your time and Shin needs you."

Her last two hours. She could spend them with Shin. *Lord, please grant me the strength to be there for Shin.* "Where is he?"

"He sleeps in his room for now. Aoki is preparing breakfast." He leaned in, his shoulder touching hers and sending waves through her frame. "Nene has laid out a special kimono for you. She will help you put it on. Rouse Shin and spend a few minutes with him, then you need to eat. Please follow what I say. Aoki and I will soon try to restore your faith."

###

Kira ran her fingers through Shin's hair again. This

simple touch gave her joy she had never known. She could not bring herself to wake him. Did he understand what would happen today? What did children understand of death? What did they know of life? For his last moments, may he enjoy peace.

Kira had found the kimono as Igami had said with Nene waiting to assist. Another patchwork kimono, this one half-gold and half-white, split vertically down the middle. Appropriate for someone caught in two worlds. Nene assisted Kira, then finished by tying the red obi behind her back. As she dressed, flashes of the accident surfaced in her thoughts. *How quickly it can end.*

Nene left the room. A few minutes later, a knock sounded at the door.

"Come in."

The door slid open. Igami smiled at her and then looked at Shin, his eyes wide. "You have not awakened him?"

"It has only been a few minutes."

"It has been thirty. You need to wake him. Now."

She nudged Shin's thin frame. "Shin, wake up."

"Okakasama, do I have to?" He remained flat on his bedding with his eyes closed.

"Yes," she answered.

Shin sat up, rubbed his eyes, and smiled at Igami. "Good morning, teacher. How are you?"

"I am well, young Shin. You should rise and go to the kitchen. I believe Master Aoki could use your help with breakfast. I need to talk with your mother."

"Yes, sir." Shin rose and helped Kira put away the bedding, then put on his slippers and left, his steps making a slap patter as he proceeded down the hall.

"He seems happy for now," Kira said.

"Yes, have you told him anything?" Igami asked.

"Nothing. He does not know what happened to his father yet. I think it best he not learn yet."

"What will you say to him?" Igami's somber tone marked a contrast to his normal personality.

"I will say that we are going to see his father and that he needs to trust me."

"Good. There is a dark blue kimono about his size in the kitchen. After breakfast, tell him to put it on and say you have a special day planned. When you are ready, take Shin to the boathouse on the lake."

His words struck like the crash into the guardrail. "Am I to drown us both? What if the magistrate wants to take us in or kill us now?"

"Then tell him you wish to have one last view of the lake with Shin."

"The magistrate will allow that?"

He stared, as if in disbelief he had to explain. "Shin is the son of a high-level samurai. They will accept your request. The magistrate will believe you wish to spare Shin pain, like any responsible parent."

"Then what?"

"I will meet you there."

Her heart swelled. Igami had a plan. "You can save us?"

"Not both of you." He dropped his gaze. "Just Shin."

That was the plan. To save Shin, she would have to die.

By drowning myself.

"Is this the only way?"

"Yes."

Water. Her greatest fear. "Igami, did the other Kira know what was about to happen?"

"She suspected, I am sure. I think her fear overcame her. I believe it is the reason she fell off the dock."

And the reason Kira was here to replace her. "What do we do now?"

"We eat," Igami said, trying to look cheerful. "Master Aoki waits for us, too. As much as I make comments about his cooking, he does some dishes very well. This meal should be good."

A last meal, and then I will probably puke.

Igami had not been wrong. Master Aoki had done a wonderful job with breakfast. Else the realization one was eating one's last meal made one enjoy the simple flavors of life.

"How is it?" Master Aoki asked.

"You put your heart into it, Master Aoki," Kira said.

His gaze flitted back between her and Igami. "Put my heart into it?"

Another confusing phrase. "It was the best breakfast I have ever eaten."

He bowed low. "At your service." He glanced up from his bow, a tear forming at the edge of his eyes. "I will miss you," he whispered.

Kira smiled, knowing it was the last time she would see him.

A bell sounded from the front door.

The magistrate. Must be time.

"Shin," Kira took a deep breath, "we are going to the lake."

"For swimming? It is cold."

"I want us to walk around for a few minutes." The bell sounded again. "Let me answer the door, then we will walk down there." She saw the blue kimono Igami mentioned earlier and pointed at it. "Put on that kimono and stay here. I will return in a few minutes."

"I will."

Kira looked for Igami, but he was no longer around. She headed to the door, her steps heavy.

The sound of pounding fists resonated in the hall.

Better hurry.

Kira slid the door open. Haseda stood there, his face petulant. She bowed low. *Must keep him happy.* "Magistrate, welcome."

No return pleasantries. Kira was beneath him now. "It is time. Where is the child?"

"He is dressing to be presentable."

"Very well." His sneer showed his disdain. "Do you have any last requests?"

"I would like to take him to the lake for one last view from the dock." She took a breath to calm her nerves. "It was a special place for him. For us. We will only be a few moments."

He frowned, as if keeping a simmering temper in check. Her mouth grew dry. Her fate was in the fickleness of the magistrate. Would he say no? Time stopped like a dammed river.

Lord, for Shin. Please.

Haseda exhaled loudly. "I grant your request. Make it quick. You have already required too much time."

Igami, it worked. "Yes, Magistrate. Thank you for your kindness."

The magistrate departed, but only to remove himself from the house. Kira knew he would watch. She headed to the kitchen.

Shin waited with a smile. "I am ready."

"Good. Let us go to the lake."

Kira held Shin's hand as the two of them headed outside and walked to the boathouse. A brisk, noisy gust blew against her. It might be the best thing. The wind would blur the magistrate's attention.

The walk down to the lake took only a few minutes. Each step felt like the anchor she knew she would soon carry.

She reached the boathouse. The raft, still tied to the dock, bobbed on the water. An anchor lay on the raft, its rope tied to a pole near the edge. Everything set. Could she go through with this?

Shin squeezed her hand. She turned and looked into his eyes. *I have to do this. For his sake.*

They entered the boathouse.

It was its own room, with another behind. Chairs to sit. A place to relax.

Igami stepped from the back room and into view.

"Teacher," Shin said, "is this a lesson?"

Igami knelt and brought his finger to his lips. "Young Shin, say nothing. Very important. You must remain quiet. Do you understand?"

Shin looked at Kira, his mouth open. "Okakasama, what is it?"

"Shin," Kira said, "I need you to be quiet and listen to Igami. Can you do that for me?"

He nodded his head. "Yes."

"Good." She looked at Igami. "What next?"

Igami moved to the corner of the room and picked up a child-sized straw figure. The figure had a blue kimono, similar to Shin's, and a mask on its face. A switch?

"That thing will work?" she asked.

He inhaled and licked his lips, as if the words might stick in his mouth. "It is our hope. The magistrate watches from a distance. He expects you to do your duty."

"Okakasama, where are you going? Where is Father?" Shin stared at her. Tears formed at the edges of his eyes.

"Shin"—Kira bit her lip to keep her tears inside—"I need you to be brave. Can you be brave for me?"

He wiped his eyes with his sleeve. "Yes."

"I have to leave. Igami will take care of you. You must do everything he says. Most important, say nothing until he says it is okay to talk."

"Where is Father?"

She exhaled slowly. "Father had to leave, too."

He rubbed his fingers in his eyes. "Will I see him soon?"

"Yes, I promise."

More tears flowed from Shin's eyes. Was there any way she could change this?

Kira hugged him and kissed his cheek.

Flashes of flight. Just like her dream. She and Shin trying to run. The magistrate catching them.

Killing them both.

That was why she was here. The previous Kira had run, costing Shin his life.

Kira needed to follow through, to save Shin.

"Why are you leaving? Is it because of Father?"

Kira sighed. He knew more than she had expected.

"Your father did the duty of Lord Oda. Now I must do the same."

"And me?"

She shook her head. "Your duty is to stay with Igami. He is your new father."

"Where will we go?"

Igami knelt and grabbed Shin's shoulders. "I will tell you in time."

"Where?"

Igami dried Shin's tears with the back of his hand. "Do not worry. Accept what is. For now, I want you to sit and pray with me. Can you do that?"

Shin nodded and moved to one corner of the boathouse. What was he thinking? His father was dead. His mother was about to die, at least the woman he knew as his mother. How did a child adjust to that?

"Any last advice, Igami?" Kira still hoped for a potential change.

"Acceptance and prayer will work for you, too."

"How do you accept?"

"Swallow water, I have heard. Less air. Less time."

"Anything else?"

He pulled out a string from under the doll's kimono. "Tie this string to your wrist. It is tied to the straw Shin. You can make it move this way. The doll is weighted, so the wind will not reveal the deception. There is a spike in its foot, so it can look like Shin is standing on the raft. Set the straw Shin next to you. Unmoor the raft and push yourself out until the pole no longer reaches the bottom. Tie the anchor to your foot, then—"

"I understand the rest." Put straw Shin on her lap, push the anchor off the boat, and go in with it. She would sink.

Shin would be safe.

"Take care of Shin. He will be all alone."

Igami leaned forward and whispered, "Do not worry. When the time is right, he will see his brother." He held a finger to his lips. "As I have said, Yutani is good with children."

So that was why Yutani was on the grounds last night. Kira gazed into Igami's eyes one last time, stepped forward, and pressed her lips against his. Ogawa was dead. She was breaking no promises. No stain on his honor. He held her tight, tasting of honey and forever. At least she would know his lips before she died.

Shin rushed forward and hugged her again. "Okakasama, do not go."

"I have to . . . for you."

"How about Lord Oda?"

"I am following the orders of a braver man. Your father. Promise me you will stay quiet. Your father is watching you now. I will be watching you, too. Always listen to Igami."

"I will."

"Thank Nene and Taka for their kindness."

Igami's face turned dark.

Kira's heart sank into her stomach. "What is it?"

"A separate order arrived to find the tea set Ogawa used yesterday and see it delivered to Lord Niwa. When they cannot deliver it, they will pay for their disobedience."

Kira looked down. The entire house.

"Do not despair, Kira of the future," Igami said. "This is their last act of faithful service to a kind master. For them, it is an honor. Time for you to leave, or the magistrate will grow suspicious."

Kira nodded. Nene and Taka would face their destiny. Time for Kira to face hers. She hugged Shin one more time and bowed to them both. She tied the fake Shin to her arm and held it against her, left through a second door that opened out on the dock, shutting it on her life here.

Kira reached the raft and set up the straw figure as instructed. She unwound the rope from its moorings and used a pole to push herself away, making sure to occasionally pull the string. It worked as Igami had said.

She peered back at the house. A figure clad in brown stood near where the tea house had once been.

The magistrate.

Could he see her? He made no move. Two more figures stood nearby. The magistrate appeared to give them no orders. Had the plan worked?

She was not done yet.

She drifted, minute by minute, a few feet by a few feet.

The wind whipped off the surface, bringing the smell of pine and sludge.

Looked far enough now.

Prayer, Igami had said.

Kira's grandmother would agree.

She sat and tied the anchor to her feet, put the doll

in her lap, and said a prayer. She hoped her grandmother would be proud.

She glanced at the water. The reflection of the other Kira looked back at her, wearing the same kimono, except the reflection's kimono was folded right side over left. The proper dress for burial. That Kira smiled and nodded as if expressing thanks and then the image faded away.

Kira looked again at the magistrate. At least she thought it was him. No one approached the boathouse. That was proof enough.

Swallow the water, Igami had said.

She took a breath, held the doll tight with one arm, and pushed the anchor off the side. Her body jerked downward. Her head struck the raft.

Reality faded into nothing.

CHAPTER NINE

Kira moved her head from side to side against her pillow. Her throbbing temple weighed on her like a brick.

"Unnh," she said.

"She's coming around," a woman's voice said.

Scents of cleaning agents filled her nose, mixed with perfume, sweat, and sterile linens. Footsteps drew nearer and familiar touches grasped each of her hands.

I'm alive. I'm alive.

Kira opened her eyes. Her mother and father were on each side of her, both beaming with happiness.

She was home. Back in her own time.

Shin, I hope you are safe.

"Where am I?"

"You're at the hospital," the unknown woman's voice said. An attractive thirtysomething woman of medium height with short brown hair and an obvious baby bump approached and looked at Kira over glasses perched on the end of her nose. "I'm Dr. Sanchez.

You're a very lucky woman."

"What happened?"

"Your car plowed through a guardrail and plunged into Lake Lanier. You've been mostly unconscious since rescuers pulled you out last night. Sometimes, you'd mumble a few things and go back to sleep. What do you remember?"

Kira sighed. "I remember nothing after the air bag deployed and I rolled. What did I say?"

The doctor looked pensive. "I don't know. I didn't understand a word of it. According to your mother, you were speaking an odd form of Japanese."

Kira turned to her mother. "You were here all the time? What did I say?"

Her mother squeezed her hand again. "Yes, I never left your side. But it was difficult to watch you. Difficult to hear. You were speaking formal. Respectful." Her eyes sparkled. "Not used to that from you."

Yes, Mama. Glad your sarcasm is back. "What did I say?"

"Something about children, battle, and sacrifice. You also talked about writing and how *hiragana* characters are written. I didn't understand everything." She smiled at her. "No matter. You're awake. You can tell me more when you feel stronger. Your father and I can rest now."

She squeezed her parents' hands again, afraid to let go. How close had she come to losing them? Or they her? Would they understand what she'd been through?

Did she understand it herself?

The doctor studied the readings on the machines. "Ms. Sakamichi, you seem to be doing better, but I recommend you rest. Holly the nurse will check on you later. As for your parents"—the doctor smiled—"I recommend they, especially your mother, get something to eat. I don't want them so tired that they faint."

The doctor left the room. Both her parents pulled chairs next to the edge of her bed. They had circles under their eyes.

"You've all been waiting up with me?" Kira asked.

Her mother pulled her chair closer. "Of course."

"Papa, have you slept?"

"I have." He pointed toward a small sofa on another wall. "The furniture here is comfortable." He patted her hand, then kissed her forehead. "Good to see you awake."

"I'm sorry to have worried you."

"The doctor said you would be fine when you woke up," her father said. "You kept mumbling, like your mother said. I heard you talk about words for *mother* and, strangely, you also mentioned Hashiba. We knew it would be soon."

"I remember Hashiba in my dreams, but I don't know what it means."

"Your grandmother was here when you said it. It made her happy. It's an old name for Toyotomi Hideyoshi. She thinks your grandfather was teaching you in his dream."

Hideyoshi. The man who succeeded Nobunaga. Perhaps.

Kira glanced down. A hospital gown had replaced her beautiful kimono. Nothing could have been done. "What did you do with my clothes?"

"They're gone," her mother said. "It was cold, and you were soaked. They had to cut them off of you and get you warm. Once that happened, a nurse washed you and put you in a gown."

"Probably for the best. The outfit would bring troubling memories." She looked at her mother. "Have you changed your clothes?"

"I gave your father a list of things to bring me from the house. A friend of mine met him there and helped him find everything."

"Why?"

"Your father's a man. He'd still be looking for things."

"That was nice of your friend."

"She was happy to do it. She's the one with the son I wanted you to meet. Nice young man. He brought his mother to the hospital."

Kira's heart fluttered. "He's here? The man you wanted to set me up with is here? How could you do that?"

"You didn't object."

"Mama, I was unconscious."

"Like I said, you didn't object."

She shook her head. "I must look horrible. Can I see a mirror?"

Her mother pulled out a compact from her purse. Kira popped it open. Gone was the more youthful, slender face and long hair of the other Kira. She was back to her full-faced self. Yesterday afternoon's makeup running across her face. "Ugh."

"What's the problem?"

"I have dark streaks on my eyes and cheeks. You thought this was fine?"

"You look beautiful."

Kira gritted her teeth and looked at the mirror again. "Oh, well, there is one bright spot. After seeing me like this, he'll never want to see me again."

"Well," her mother started, "you'll see him at least one more time."

Kira's breath caught in her throat. "Why?"

"He went out to get coffee for us. Should be back any minute."

A knock sounded from the outside. "Hello, anyone here?" a man's voice asked.

"We're here," her mother said.

A man walked in carrying a tray with steaming cups. Beautiful soft eyes, rugged shoulders, and bald. Kira's mouth dropped open.

Igami?

"You know my name?" the man asked.

"I . . . I don't think I said anything."

His smile grew wider. "You mouthed the word *Igami* like you did." He handed the coffee to her parents. "Though I guess your mother or father might have mentioned my name."

"We said nothing." Kira's mother turned to her. "His mother and I are childhood friends. However, it has been a long time since we've seen each other. Too long. She came back into my life at the right time."

"Maybe I heard it while I was sleeping," Kira said. "Maybe I met you once before." Her face grew flushed. She could never explain.

"What is it?" Igami asked.

"Oh, nothing." Kira shook her head. "I guess I wasn't expecting…"

"You weren't expecting someone your mother is trying to set you up with to show up in the hospital."

"It's nothing against you." She glanced down, her stomach churning. "Streaked makeup and a hospital gown. Not my best."

He laughed again. "You look fine to me, particularly given what you've been through. As for me"—he ran his hand over his head—"I normally have hair." He held out his hand. "My name is Stephen. Nice to meet you."

"Kira." She took his hand. His touch was light yet firm.

And familiar.

"So why don't you have hair?"

"I lost a bet on the Michigan-Ohio State football game." His gaze rose as he paused. "This is the result.

It's fine. It will grow back. However, I think the football team is still doomed."

Memories of the Igami she left behind appeared in her mind. "It's not too bad now. You should think about keeping it."

"Your father and I are going for a walk," her mother said. "I haven't left the room much. Be back soon." She kissed Kira's forehead. "You're in capable hands."

Kira shook her head. Leaving her here alone with a man she just met. Mama was nuts.

Stephen pulled up a chair next to the bed. "I'm glad to see you're okay."

She stared at him. "You don't even know me."

"Yes, but I hope to learn more about you."

"You could have at least brought me coffee." She did her best to smile, hoping he would see her comment as a joke, but an effort to sit up caused her pain.

"You weren't awake when I left," he whispered as he smiled back. "Didn't guess you'd want some. I haven't drunk from mine yet. You can have it."

"No, thanks. I'll deal without it for now. But when my parents return, could you?"

"I'll be happy to. If I get you some, will you tell me more about that dream you were having?"

Kira glanced toward the ceiling. How much could she tell him? It felt so real. No one would believe her. She pressed her hands against the bed and pushed herself into a sitting position. Jabs of pain pinged her temples. She touched the left side of her head. The bump was the same in both time periods. She would endure.

"It's probably not good to strain yourself yet," he said.

"I need to move. On second thought, can I take a sip of your coffee?"

He handed it to her. "It's yours. I hope it's warm

enough for you."

"I survived a plunge into a lake. I'm sure I can handle it."

"So what was the dream?"

She paused and took a sip. Where to begin? "I dreamed I was back in time, around the sixteenth century in Japan, and I was a consort to one of Nobunaga's top samurai. I had a child who had difficulty learning his characters. A Buddhist monk in the dream worked with my child to help him overcome it."

"Very detailed for a dream"—he raised his eyebrows as he tilted his head to the side—"and an interesting coincidence."

"Why is it a coincidence?"

"I work with children with dyslexia. My specialty is in using foreign languages. Greek is sometimes used to help children deal with their challenges. Some teachers use Japanese and Chinese as well. The characters are visual, stimulating, and fun for children."

A guy who smiles about helping children. Not bad. "How did you get interested in this?"

"I come from a long line of educators. Every generation, at least one member of my family is in education, even going back a few centuries in Japan."

"They were always teachers?"

He laughed. "If you go back far enough, they were Buddhist monks like in your dream. Another reason for my surprise."

I'm not surprised. "So in every generation, someone in the family became a monk?"

"For a while, yes. Mostly children following in their parents' footsteps."

"I'd love to hear more about it."

"No." He smiled. "You don't want to take that chance: I've been told I get too excited when I talk about my family history and that I can't shut up."

The scent of flowers caught her attention. An enormous bouquet sat on a nearby table. "How beautiful. Did my mother do that?"

He shook his head. "From your office. Someone named Tanner brought them early this morning."

Tanner. Damn. Another guy showing up. Wrong time to explain things. What did Igami think of that? "That was nice of him. Did he say anything?"

"Your team has been notified and everyone is thinking of you. Also that management says to take your time on recovery."

"I wonder how the office knew quickly."

"Your parents wondered the same thing. Company documents in your car. Calling the company was the first call the police made to locate your family."

I should have known. "Makes sense."

"Tanner's wife came with him. She said that she would prepare a few meals for you once you get home."

Tanner's wife came? Phew. "That was nice of her. I'll have to text him when I find my phone. If I find my phone."

"It was found. My mother put it in a bowl of uncooked rice. She has been trying to assist your mother in whatever way she can."

"I am grateful," she said as she took another sip of coffee. "What were you saying about your family?"

"Just warning you I talk too much when I talk about them. You don't want me to start."

Kira tried to push herself up farther. "I'll take that chance. I've been told I clean up well."

He smiled widely with a silent laugh. "Once you're out, I'd love to meet up with you. For now, I'll keep it down to one story."

"Make it the best one, please."

"I will. An ancestor of mine helped fake the deaths of two children of a condemned samurai in order to save their lives. The children were raised in different monasteries to hide their parentage. One child supposedly had reading difficulties but grew up to be a teacher himself."

"Sounds wonderful. I can't wait to hear more."

"That is the good part. Unfortunately, there is sadness in the story. Two servants smuggled out the samurai's most valuable items, a coveted tea set and other things, to fund the children's expenses. They paid with their lives."

Kira's heart grew heavy. *Nene and Taka, God bless you both.* "Save the full story for when I am stronger."

"I will. Do you know what you will do when you get out of the hospital?"

"Not yet, but I know one change I will make."

"What's that?"

She recalled the face of the other Kira. "I plan to let my hair grow long."

EPILOGUE

Saturday night had not come quickly enough.

The doctor had released Kira two days later, wanting to keep her for observation. Her mother had moved in for a few days to ensure Kira was okay, fussing over her and driving her crazy. Tanner's wife had brought several days of meals as promised. Her mother had said it was unnecessary, but Tanner's wife had said that Kira's mother needed her rest as well.

Her mother had finally let up when Kira had given her the news she craved. Kira had made a date with Stephen.

The joy on her mother's face made Kira happy.

Stephen had taken her to Atoneta's, her new favorite Italian restaurant. When Stephen had mentioned Italian, Kira had imagined romantic as opposed to the family crowd that was there. The garlic and spice scents had made her mouth water before she'd taken her seat. The pasta and rolls had guaranteed her return.

She hadn't wanted the night to end. Unfortunately,

she tired easily. Had since she'd come home from the hospital.

"How was everything?" Stephen asked as they stopped at her door.

"It was wonderful."

"We still have time. It may be too soon, but we can still do the Lake Lanier Christmas lights tour tonight."

An apprehensive tingle flowed across her skin. She wanted to go. She just wasn't ready for Lanier. "How about next weekend? I'll be ready for Lanier by then."

Stephen's smile curled her toes. "I can't wait."

She leaned forward and kissed him, his soft lips teasing hers. The feelings from Japan rushed back like a wave.

"If I didn't tell you before," she said, "your family story was amazing. Your relative sounds brave."

"Thank you," he said. "I hope to see you again soon."

Her entire body tingled and she kissed him again. "Me, too."

"Before I leave though, I have one question."

"What's that?"

Stephen's lips pressed into a thin line. "You never told me why there was a large lump of straw in your car."

Kira smiled. "One day. Soon."

The End

HISTORICAL/CULTURAL NOTES

I've endeavored to make my stories as historically accurate as possible. Please email me with any mistakes you find. Historical and cultural elements are listed below on a chapter-by-chapter basis. Definitions of specific words are listed in the Glossary in the next section.

Chapter One

Taiga Drama - A year-long historical drama produced each year since 1963 by NHK (Japanese PBS).

Yoshitsune – The 2005 Taiga drama about Minamoto no Yoshitsune, famous general and younger brother of Minamoto no Yoritomo, founder of Japan's feudal system of government. The episode involving the Battle of Dan-no-ura, where the young emperor jumps overboard, is Episode 35.

Battle of Dan-no-ura - The 1185 climactic sea battle fought in the Shimonoseki Strait between the Minamoto and Taira clans resulted in a defeat of the Taira and the establishment of Minamoto clan as the rulers of Japan. The grandmother of the emperor jumped into the sea with the six-year-old emperor, Antoku, to drown both of them.

Chapter Two

Location in Japan – The Japanese lake in the story is Lake Hamana, which was within Oda Nobunaga's domain at the time. Though still called a lake, Lake Hamana is connected to the ocean, owing to an earthquake in 1498.

96 • *Historical/Cultural Notes*

Eigamura – Kyoto-based tourist attraction that is also an actual movie set used for the shooting of historical dramas set during the Edo Period (1603-1868) under the Tokugawa Shogunate. Eigamura translates to *movie village*.

The usage of "-san" – Japan's most common term of address evolved from "-sama" in the seventeenth century. The term "-chan" appeared in the nineteenth century. For more information, I recommend the reader search online for the book *Learning from Shogun*. It's a free download and is a compilation by a group of Japanese history professors on what James Clavell gets wrong in his book *Shogun*.

Tenshō Era – The period from July 1573 through December 1592.

Chapter Three

Famous Battles of Oda Nobunaga – When Kira is puzzling out what she knows about Oda Nobunaga, she first recalls a battle she names the "one with the guns." Kira's reference is vague as it matches her recall of what her grandfather taught her. Nobunaga was an early adopter of guns, but one battle in this time period stands out in Japanese history. This battle is the Battle of Nagashino. It occurred in the summer of 1575 and pitted the forces of Oda Nobunaga and Tokugawa Ieyasu vs. the forces of the Takeda Katsuyori.

Kira also mentions the "Buddhist temple in Kyoto." This refers to two things and again shows the state of Kira's memory. The first is the Siege of Mount Hiei in early fall of 1571, pitting Nobunaga's forces against a sect of warrior monks northeast of Kyoto. The second was the assassination of Nobunaga at Honnō-ji Temple in June of 1582.

Large stone Buddhas of Nara and Kamakura – This is a reference to the two famous Buddha statues that people think about with regard to Japan. The one in Nara is indoor, was constructed in the eighth century, and is the world's largest bronze Buddha statue. The one in Kamakura is outdoors and was constructed in the thirteenth century. The building that housed the outdoor one was taken out by a tsunami in 1498 and it's been outside ever since. The tsunami resulted from the earthquake that was mentioned in the previous section that connected Lake Hamana with the ocean.

Dyslexia in Japan - For Japanese children with dyslexia, the character さ (romanized as *sa* and pronounced *sa*) can be switched to ち (romanized as both *ti* and *chi* and pronounced *chee*).

Japanese bathing practices - The Japanese are known for their attention to cleanliness, but it would have required a lot of heating water and servants to make a bath possible. Instead, people tried to clean themselves at home the best they could and then have baths when possible, most likely at a Buddhist temple. (This was a source of donations for temples.) The sauna-like room in the house was a stretch. Such rooms existed, but it is debatable if Ogawa would have had one.

Teeth blackening – A practice that went on in Japan for many centuries, though the reasons why varied. In the time period of this novella, it was seen among adults, sometimes as an indication of status. It was also used by preteen daughters of military figures to indicate the beginning of adulthood.

98 • *Historical/Cultural Notes*

Walnut-scented perfume – A Jesuit missionary from the period remarked in a book that Japanese women reek of oil. Walnut, cloves, camelia, and sesame were mentioned by the book's translator as possibilities.

Medieval Japanese birthing practices – Kira's flashbacks on Mitsuyono's birth are a combination of comments from a representative of the Japanese Midwives Association, an NHK (Japanese PBS) special on medieval birthing practices, and some Japanese shows. Per the Midwives Association, women in 1600 delivered in a sitting position with the help of a *koshikakae*, a word that is a combination of *koshi* (lower back) and *kakae* (to hold in the arms). A poor woman would have visited a local woman for the birth while a rich woman would have given birth in a building on the property.

    One interesting fact mentioned in the NHK special is that women were kept awake and seated for seven days after the birth to protect against both health problems and demons. Fr. Luis Frois, a sixteenth-century Jesuit missionary in Japan, stated that Japanese women remain seated for twenty days after birth.

Japanese bedding – The beginnings of bedding that resembles the modern futon started possibly around the mid-sixteenth century, though sources vary on this topic. Centuries prior, Japanese people slept on straw or woven straw mats. People began stacking these mats and this eventually became the tatami floors. Around the mid-sixteenth century, thin cotton bedding appeared along with quilt-kimono hybrids that evolved into quilts.

Chapter Four

The Battle of the Tedori River – I've always been

fascinated by this battle. Beginning in the latter half of the sixteenth century, three individuals united Japan: Oda Nobunaga, Toyotomi Hideyoshi, and Tokugawa Ieyasu. (Last name first per Japanese convention.) Nobunaga began the process, uniting roughly half of the country before his assassination in 1582. Hideyoshi avenged Nobunaga, then clashed with the other generals and rose to power. He conquered the rest of the country, but his son was too young to rule when Hideyoshi died in 1598. Ieyasu eventually usurped power, establishing a family succession that lasted until the nineteenth century.

So why does that make this battle of interest?

In November 1577, the forces of Oda Nobunaga met the forces of another warlord, Uesugi Kenshin, at the Tedori River. Nobunaga's forces, armed with guns and superior numbers, figured to overwhelm Kenshin's forces. However, rain and the river negated Nobunaga's advantage in arms and Kenshin's army routed Nobunaga's, a group that included both Hideyoshi and Ieyasu, though some sources place Hideyoshi elsewhere at the time of battle. (Niwa Nagahide, the samurai who appears in this story, was also at the battle.)

For reasons no one knows, Kenshin's forces allowed Nobunaga's to retreat. Given the hatred of Nobunaga by his rivals, any other *daimyo* (feudal warlord) would have pressed the advantage against Nobunaga, hoping to eliminate him. I've always wondered, though, what would have happened had Kenshin pursued. He could possibly have eliminated Hideyoshi and Ieyasu in addition to Nobunaga. At the very least, Kenshin could have weakened Nobunaga to the point where someone could have taken advantage of the situation.

Whoever ruled, it would not have been Kenshin. The daimyo died a year later in 1578, reportedly from cancer though some legends assert that Kenshin fell due to a ninja assassination. With two potential successors, the Uesugi clan warred internally, eventually ceding territory to the forces of Nobunaga.

Dyslexia in Japan – For Japanese children with dyslexia, the character お (romanized as *o* and pronounced *oh*) can be switched to あ (romanized as *a* and pronounced *ah*).

Chapter Five

Potters from Seto – Oda Nobunaga convinced some famous potters who lived near him and specialized in Chinese-style pottery to move to an area under his control and begin producing their wares. While those potters did produce Chinese-style goods after they moved, they also began producing a Japanese-style appearance that grew in popularity, including etched paintings under the glaze.

Tōdai-ji – This is the name of the famous temple in Nara that houses the large indoor Buddha previously mentioned.

Southern Barbarians – The Portuguese traders, the first Europeans to visit Japan, were regarded as barbarians as they were illiterate, cursed, ate with their hands, and didn't bathe. The Southern portion arose as European traders always approached Japan from the south.

Rice Country – The word *Beikoku*, the original Japanese term for the US, arose from the four-character Chinese phonetic spelling for America. The character that represents *me* in the Chinese term means rice. The character has several pronunciations in Japanese, including *bei*.

Chapter Six

Shin-chan – A famous manga about a mischievous five-year-old Japanese boy named Shinnosuke. Better known as "Crayon Shin-chan."

Kirakira – The word is defined in the glossary as an onomatopoeic word to mean glitter, twinkle, or sparkle. However, I'm mentioning it here as its usage is dissimilar from English. The Japanese language depends much more heavily on onomatopoeia than English does.

Chapter Seven

Burning of the tea house – This incident is inspired by a real event. One of the generals who fought Toyotomi Hideyoshi for succession was Shibata Katsuie. Facing defeat, Katsuie and his wife, who was also Nobunaga's younger sister, committed *seppuku*, ritual suicide. Katsuie served as his wife's second and also set fire to the castle. Other servants willingly died as well.

Chapter Eight

None

Chapter Nine

University of Michigan – University of Michigan Press has a sizable Japanese history offering (for those interested). No comment on football.

Dyslexia and Japanese characters – Japan actually has a low incidence of dyslexia and Japanese and Chinese characters can be used to help those with dyslexia.

Hashiba Hideyoshi – Samurai often went through name changes in their lives for any number of reasons. Though remembered historically as Toyotomi Hideyoshi, he did not have that name until Japan's Imperial Court awarded him the Toyotomi name in 1586. In the 1570s, he was known as Hashiba Hideyoshi. His earliest name, though, was Kinoshita Tōkichirō.

Epilogue

The historical Kira – With straw being in the car, it suggests that the incident was possibly real and not just a vivid dream. This would mean that the historical Kira died in Lake Hamana . . . or maybe not. One source of the author's does suggest that Lake Hamana is haunted by a female ghost that pulls souls to the bottom. We shall see.

GLOSSARY OF TERMS

- chan – A term of address used for children. Also a term of affection within a family.

futon – A traditional bedroll that can be folded and stored daily.

hahaue – Mother

kana – The two syllabaries of the Japanese language. One syllabary, *hiragana*, is used for Japanese words and can be used by itself or with the kanji characters. The other syllabary, *katakana*, is used to pronounce foreign words.

kanji – The modified versions of the borrowed Chinese characters used in Japanese writing.

kataginu – A vest with winglike shoulders worn by samurai.

ki o tsukete – "Take care" / "Be careful."

kimono – A traditional Japanese garment that resembles a loose robe.

kirakira – An onomatopoeic word that indicates to glitter, twinkle, or sparkle.

Kirishitans – The Japanese word for Christians.

okaasan – Mother

okakasama – Mother. The appropriate term of address in a samurai family.

- sama – A term of address that shows respect to someone who is of elevated rank.

- san – The most common title. It can mean "Mr.," "Mrs.," "Ms.," and "Miss."

seppuku – ritual suicide

tatami – A straw mat floor covering where the length is twice the width. Sizes vary by region but are around six feet by three feet.

tokonoma – A recessed space in a Japanese house typically used for displaying such things as flower arrangements or hanging scrolls.

BIBLIOGRAPHY

My Japanese history library is voluminous. The list below suggests references that readers might enjoy for further historical study.

Cooper, Michael S.J. (Editor) – *They Came to Japan: An Anthology of European Reports on Japan, 1543 – 1640.* Reprinted in 1995 by the Center for Japanese Studies, The University of Michigan.

Frois, Louis S.J. – *Topsy-Turvy 1585: The Short Version.* Translated from Portuguese by Robin D. Gill. Published in 2005 by Paraverse Press.

Smith, Henry (Editor) - *Learning from Shogun: Japanese History and Western Fantasy.* Distributed by the Japan Society, New York.

Turnbull, Stephen – *The Samurai and the Sacred.* Published 2006 by Osprey Publishing.

Other Sources:

The Costume Museum – Located in Kyoto, the Costume Museum provides a history of clothing throughout Japan's history and its site is in English as well as Japanese. Check out www.iz2.or.jp/english/.

Samurai Archives at www.samuraipodcast.com is an excellent source of Japanese history. The author used information learned in the podcasts but never consulted the creators directly.

ACKNOWLEDGMENTS

I thank you reading my novella, *A Second Chance*. As I mentioned, the story was initially published under the title *Second Chances* and was part of an anthology to support a school in Atlanta for children with dyslexia. Every story in that anthology contained a reference to dyslexia, and this is the reason dyslexia is part of this story. The anthology still exists under the title *Love & Grace Boxed Set* and can be purchased in that form.

Though Kira is now back in the present, I've decided it will not be her only trip and am considering when might Shinnosuke need his mother's help again. At this point, Kira will be needed at least twice.

Thank you to Ciara Knight and Lindi Peterson for inviting me on the original project. Given that our writing primarily targets different readerships, the chance to work with the two of you was one I wasn't going to pass up.

Thank you to Dianna Love and Tina Radcliffe for your continued willingness to answer this writer's questions on every imaginable topic.

Thank you to JC Kang for story development and cover discussions.

Thank you to Kim W. Moore and E. A. McDermott for beta reads and suggestions. Thank you to Lindi Peterson and Kayla Tocco for their review of the original manuscript and suggested changes.

Thank you to Stuart Iles of the Japanese history website www.rekishinihon.com for his review of the historical aspects of the story.

Thanks to my online group, Authors of Asian Novels, for your continued support, research answers, and good wishes.

Thank you to my online group, Indie Cover Project, for cover review and suggestions.

Thank you to Ohio Kimono for your lengthy discussion and source suggestions on how my heroine would be dressed.

Thank you to Holly Sturges, childhood friend and nurse, for explaining to me what would have happened to a patient who came into a hospital the way Kira did. Hope you like being a character.

Thank you to Kendra Harouff for discussions on both Lake Lanier and makeup practices when you've got a date after work.

Thank you to Dr. Tomoko Kitagawa for answering on how moms would be addressed in a samurai family.

Thank you to Yuki Sekiya of the Japanese Midwives Association for your notes on medieval Japan birthing practices.

Thank you to Susan Spann for cover and Japan-related research discussions.

Continued thanks to the many Japanese historians whose works I read to ensure my details are correct.

Thank you to Jason Kinsey of the Arrowsmith School in Toronto for his comments on the usage of Japanese and Chinese characters in working with children with dyslexia for the original manuscript.

Thank you to Officer Tom Carreiro for his assistance in the mechanics of auto accidents for the original manuscript. For this revised version, I flipped the vehicle for added tension.

Thank you to Michelle Semones of the University of Michigan's School of Education for researching the university's education degrees.

Thank you to Carl Creasman, history professor at Valencia College, for continually inspiring me to up my game on my knowledge of Japanese history.

Thank you to the unnamed hostess at Atoneta's who confirmed what a Saturday night crowd is like for the original manuscript. (We always do take out.)

Please note that any historical or technical mistakes in this book are the fault of the author.

Lastly, thank you to my wife, Motoyo, and my sons, Andrew and Christopher, for putting up with me when I'm writing. A special thanks again to Motoyo for the evening we spent driving around Lake Lanier with me to figure out the best place to stage an accident.

ABOUT THE AUTHOR

Walt Mussell lives in the Atlanta area with his wife and two sons. He works for a well-known corporation and writes in his spare time. Walt primarily writes historicals, with a focus on Japan, an interest he gained in the four years he lived there.

Please visit his website at www.waltmussell.com. Please follow him on Twitter at @wmussell and on Instagram at @authorwaltmussell. Please also check out his Facebook page at "Walt Mussell – Author" and check out his YouTube channel by searching for Walt Mussell to see his videos on Japanese Christian history.

Made in the USA
Columbia, SC
05 September 2021